Rob of the Bowl

A Legend of St. Inigoe's

Vol. I

by

John Pendleton Kennedy

Double9 BOOKS

Rob of the Bowl

A Legend of St. Inigoe's
Vol. I

by John Pendleton Kennedy

ISBN: 978-93-62766-16-8

Published by

DOUBLE 9 BOOKS
2/13-B, Ansari Road
Daryaganj, New Delhi – 110002
info@double9books.com
www.double9books.com
Tel. 011-40042856

ABOUT THE AUTHOR

John Pendleton Kennedy was an American novelist, lawyer, and Whig politician who served as United States Secretary of the Navy from July 26, 1852 to March 4, 1853, during President Millard Fillmore's administration, and as a U.S. Representative from Maryland's 4th congressional district, where he encouraged the United States government to study, adopt, and implement the telegraph. Kennedy, a lawyer who became a lobbyist and director of the Baltimore and Ohio Railroad, also served in the Maryland General Assembly for numerous times, eventually becoming Speaker in 1847. Kennedy later led the drive to abolish slavery in Maryland, which, as a non-Confederate state, was not impacted by the Emancipation Proclamation and required a state statute to free slaves within its borders and prohibit the practice's continuation. Kennedy also promoted religious tolerance and expanded research into Maryland history. He contributed to the preservation or establishment of Historic St. Mary's City (the site of Maryland's colonial founding and the birthplace of religious freedom in America), St. Mary's College of Maryland (then St. Mary's Female Seminary), the Peabody Library (now part of Johns Hopkins University), and the Peabody Conservatory of Music.

CONTENTS

PREFACE

The tale related in the following pages refers to a period in the history of Maryland, which has heretofore been involved in great obscurity,—many of the most important records connected with it having been lost to public inspection in forgotten repositories, where they have crumbled away under the touch of time. To the persevering research of the accomplished Librarian of the State—a gentleman whose dauntless, antiquarian zeal and liberal scholarship are only surpassed by the enlightened judgment with which he discharges the functions of his office—we are indebted for the rescue of the remnant of these memorials of by-gone days, from the oblivion to which the carelessness of former generations had consigned them. Many were irrecoverable; and it was the fate of the gentleman referred to, to see them fall into dust at the moment that the long estranged light first glanced upon them.

To some of those which have been saved from this wreck, the author is indebted for no small portion of the materials of his story. In his endeavour to illustrate these passages in the annals of the state, it is proper for him to say that he has aimed to perform his task with historical fidelity. If he has set in harsher lights than may be deemed charitable some of the actors in these scenes, or portrayed in lineaments of disparagement or extenuation, beyond their deserts, the partisans on either side in that war of intolerance which disfigured the epoch of this tale, it was apart from his purpose. As a native of the state he feels a prompt sensibility to the fame of her Catholic founders, and, though differing from them in his faith, cherishes the remembrance of their noble endeavours to establish religious freedom, with the affection due to what he believes the most wisely planned and honestly executed scheme of society which at that era, at least, was to be found in the annals of mankind. In the temper inspired by this sentiment, these volumes have been given to the public, and are now respectfully inscribed to The State of Maryland, by one who takes the deepest interest in whatever concerns her present happiness or ancient renown.

THE AUTHOR.

Baltimore, Dec. 1, 1838.

CHAPTER I

No more thy glassy brook reflects the day,
But choked with sedges, works its weedy way;
Along thy glades a solitary guest,
The hollow-sounding bittern guards its nest;
Amidst thy desert walks the lapwing flies,
And tires their echoes with unvaried cries.
Sunk are thy bowers in shapeless ruin all,
And the long grass o'ertops the mould'ring wall.

The Deserted Village.

It is now more than one hundred and forty-four years since the ancient capital of Maryland was shorn of its honours, by the removal of the public offices, and, along with them, the public functionaries, to Annapolis. The date of this removal, I think, is recorded as of the year of grace sixteen hundred and ninety-four. The port of St. Mary's, up to that epoch, from the first settlement of the province, comprehending rather more than three score years, had been the seat of the Lord Proprietary's government. This little city had grown up in hard-favoured times, which had their due effect in leaving upon it the visible tokens of a stunted vegetation: it waxed gnarled and crooked, as it perked itself upward through the thorny troubles of its existence, and might be likened to the black jack, which yet retains a foothold in this region,—a scrubby, tough and hardy mignon of the forest, whose elder day of crabbed luxuriance affords a sour comment upon the nurture of its youth.

Geographers are aware that the city of St. Mary's stood on the left bank of the river which now bears the same name (though of old it was called St. George's,) and which flows into the Potomac at the southern extremity of the state of Maryland, on the western side of the Chesapeake Bay, at a short distance westward from Point Lookout: but the very spot where the old city stood is known only to a few,—for the traces of the early residence of the Proprietary government have nearly faded away from the knowledge of this generation. An astute antiquarian eye, however, may define the site of the town by the few scattered bricks which the ploughshare has mingled with the ordinary tillage of the fields. It may be determined, still more visibly, by the mouldering and shapeless ruin of the ancient State House, whose venerable remains,—I relate it with a blush—have been pillaged, to furnish building materials for an unsightly church, which now obtrusively presents its mottled, mortar-stained and shabby front to the view of the visiter, immediately beside the wreck of this early monument of the founders of Maryland. Over these ruins a storm-shaken and magnificent mulberry, aboriginal, and cotemporary with the settlement of the province, yet rears its shattered and topless trunk, and daily distils upon the sacred relics at its foot, the dews of heaven,—an august and brave old mourner to the departed companions of its prime. There is yet another memorial in the family tomb of the Proprietary, whose long-respected and holy repose, beneath the scant shade of the mulberry, has, within twenty years past, been desecrated by a worse than Vandal outrage, and whose lineaments may now with difficulty be followed amidst the rubbish produced by this violation.

These faded memorials tell their story like honest chroniclers. And a brave story it is of hardy adventure, and manly love of freedom! The scattered bricks, all moulded in the mother-land, remind us of the launching of the bark, the struggle with the unfamiliar wave, the array of the wonder-stricken savage, and the rude fellowship of the first meeting. They recall the hearths whose early fires gleamed upon the visage of the bold cavalier, while the deep, unconquerable faith of religion, and the impassioned instincts of the Anglo-Saxon devotion to liberty, were breathed by household groups, in customary household terms. They speak of sudden alarms, and quick arming for battle;—of stout resolve, and still stouter achievement. They tell of the victory won, and quiet gradually confirmed,—and of the increasing rapture as, day by day, the settler's hopes were converted into realities, when he saw the wilderness put forth the blossoms of security and comfort.

The river penetrates from the Potomac some twelve miles inland, where it terminates in little forked bays which wash the base of the woody hills. St. George's Island stretches half across its mouth, forming a screen by which the course of the Potomac is partly concealed from view. From this island, looking northward, up St. Mary's river, the eye rests upon a glittering sheet of water about a league in breadth, bounded on either shore by low meadow-grounds and cultivated fields girt with borders of forest; whilst in the distance, some two leagues upward, interlocking promontories, with highlands in their rear, and cedar-crowned cliffs and abrupt acclivities which shut in the channel, give to the river the features of a lake. St. Inigoe's creek, flowing into the river upon the right hand, along the base of these cliffs, forms by its southern shore a flat, narrow and grass-clad point, upon which the ancient Jesuit House of the patron saint whose name distinguishes the creek, throws up, in sharp relief, its chateau-like profile, together with its windmill, its old trees, barns and cottages,—the whole suggesting a resemblance to a strip of pasteboard scenery on a prolonged and slender base line of green.

When the voyager from the island has trimmed his sail and reached the promontories which formed his first perspective, the river, now reduced to a gun-shot in width, again opens to his view a succession of little bays, intercepted by more frequent headlands and branching off into sinuous creeks that lose themselves in the hills. Here and there, amongst these creeks, a slender beach of white sand separates from its parent flood a pool, which reposes like a mirror in the deep forest; and all around, high hills sweep down upon these placid lakes, and disclose half-embowered cottages, whose hoary roofs and antique forms turn the musings of the spectator to the palmy days of the Lord Proprietary.

A more enchanting landscape than St. Mary's river,—a lovelier assemblage of grassy bank and hoary grove, upland slope, cliff, cot and strand, of tangled brake and narrow bay, broad, seaward road-stead and air-suspended cape, may not be found beneath the yearly travel of the sun!

The ancient city was situated nearly two miles beyond the confluence of St. Inigoe's creek, upon a spacious level plain which maintained an elevation of some fifty feet above the river. The low-browed, double-roofed and cumbrous habitations of the towns-people were scattered at random over this plain, forming snug and pleasant groups for a painter's eye, and deriving an air of competence and comfort from the gardens and bowers in which they were sheltered. The State House stood at the upper extremity of the town, upon a cedar-clad headland which, by an abrupt descent, terminated in a long, flat, sandy point, that reached almost half across the river. In regard to this building, tradition—which I find to be somewhat inclined to brag of its glory—affirms it to have been constructed in the shape of a cross, looking towards the river, with walls thick enough to resist cannon, and perilous steep roofs, from the top of the chief of which shot up a spire, whereon was impaled a dolphin with a crooked, bifurcated tail. A wooden quay and warehouse on the point showed this to be the seat of trade, and a crescent-shaped bay or indentation between this and a similar headland at the lower extremity of the town, constituted the anchorage or harbour for the scant shipping of the port.

The State House looked rearward over the town common,—a large space of open ground, at the farther end of which, upon the border of a marshy inlet, covered with bulrushes and cat-tails, stood a squat, sturdy and tight little gaol, supported,—to use the military phrase,—on one flank by a pillory and stocks, and on the other by an implement of government which has gone out of fashion in our day, but which found favour with our ancestors as an approved antidote to the prevalent distemper of an unnecessary or too clamorous loquacity in their dames—a ducking stool, that hung suspended over a pool of sufficient depth for the most obstinate case that might occur.

Without wearying my reader with too much description, I shall content myself with referring to but two or three additional particulars as necessary to my future purpose: a Catholic chapel devoted to St. Ignatius, the patron of the province, in humble and unostentatious guise, occupied, with its appurtenances, a few acres in the centre of the plain, a short distance from that confine of the city which lay nearest to St. Inigoe's; and in the opposite quarter, not far from the State House, a building of much more pretension, though by no means so neat, had been erected for the service of the Church of England, which was then fast growing into the ascendant. On one of the streets leading to the beach was the market house, surrounded by its ordinaries and ale-houses: and lastly, in the year **1681**, to which this description refers, a little hostelry of famous report, known by the sign of "The Crow and Archer," and kept by Master Garret Weasel, stood on the water's edge, at the foot of the bank below the State House, on a piece of level ground looking out upon the harbour, where the traveller may still find a luxuriant wilderness of pear trees, the scions of a notable ancestor which, tradition says, the aforesaid Garret planted with his own hand.

The country around St. Mary's bore, at the period I have designated, the same broad traces of settlement and cultivation which belong to it at the present day. For many miles the scene was one of varied field and forest, studded over with dwellings and farm yards. The settlements had extended across the neck of land to the Chesapeake, and along both shores of St. Mary's river to the Potomac. This open country was diversified by woodland, and enlivened every where by the expanse of navigable water which reflected sun and sky, grove and field and lowly cottage in a thousand beautiful lights. Indeed, all the maritime border of the province, comprehending Calvert, St. Mary's and Charles, as well as the counties on the opposite shore of the Chesapeake, might be said, at this date, to be in a condition of secure and prosperous habitation. The great ocean forest had receded some hundred miles westward from St. Mary's. The region of country comprising the present county of Anne Arundel, as well as Cecil and the Isle of Kent, was a frontier already settled with numerous tenants of the Lord Proprietary. All westward from this was the birthright of the stern Sasquesahannoch, the fierce Shenandoah, and their kindred men of the woods.

They are gone! Like shadows have these men of might sunk on the earth. They, their game, their wigwams, their monuments, their primeval forests,—yea, even their graves, have flitted away in this spectral flight. Saxon and Norman, bluff Briton and heavy Suabian inherit the land. And in its turn, well-a-day! our pragmatical little city hath departed. Not all its infant glory, nor its manhood's bustle, its walls, gardens and bowers,—its warm housekeeping, its gossiping burghers, its politics and its factions,—not even its prolific dames and gamesome urchins could keep it in the upper air until this our day. Alas, for the vaulting pride of the village, the vain glory of the city, and the metropolitan boast! St. Mary's hath sunk to the level of Tyre and Sidon, Balbec and Palmyra! She hath become trackless, tokenless.

I have wandered over the blank field where she sank down to rest. It was a book whose characters I could scarce decipher. I asked for relics of the departed. The winter evening tale told by father to son, and the written legend, more durable than monument of marble, have survived to answer my question, when brick and tile, hearth and tomb have all vanished from the quest of the traveller.

What I have gathered from these researches will occupy my reader through the following pages.

CHAPTER II

A train-band captain eke was he.

John Gilpin.

At the extremity of the cape or headland which formed the lower or more seaward point of the crescent-shaped harbour, was erected the Fort of St. Mary's, where it threatened equal defiance to such as might meditate disturbance either by sea or land. A few hundred paces in the rear of the fort, stood the ample dwelling-house of the Lord Proprietary with its gables, roofs, chimneys and spires, sharply defined against the eastern sky. A massive building of dark brick, two stories in height, and penetrated by narrow windows, looking forth, beyond the fort, upon the river, constituted the chief member or main body of the mansion. This was capped by a wooden, balustraded parapet, terminating, at each extremity, in a scroll like the head of a violin, and, in the middle, sustaining an entablature that rose to a summit on which was mounted a weathercock. From this central structure, right and left, a series of arcades, corridors, and vestibules served to bring into line a range of auxiliary or subordinate buildings of grotesque shapes, of which several were bonneted like haycocks—the array terminating, on one flank, in a private chapel surmounted by a cross, and, on the other, in a building of similar size but of different figure, which was designed and sometimes used for a banqueting room. The impression produced on the observer, by this orderly though not uniform mass of building, with its various offices for household comfort, was not displeasing to his sense of rural beauty, nor, from its ample range and capacious accommodation, did it fail to enhance his opinion of the stateliness and feudal importance, as well as of the hospitality of the Lord Proprietary. The armorial bearings of the Baltimore family, emblazoned on a shield of free-stone, were built into the pediment of an arched brick porch which shaded the great hall door. In the rear of the buildings, a circular sweep of wall and paling reached as far as a group of stables, kennels and sheds. Vanward the same kind of enclosures, more ornate in their fashion, shut in a grassy court, to which admission was gained through a heavy iron gate swung between square, stuccoed pillars, each of which was surmounted by a couchant lion carved in stone. Ancient trees shaded the whole mass of dwelling-house, court and stable, and gave to the place both a lordly and comfortable aspect. It was a pleasant group of roof and bower, of spire and tree to look upon from the city, towards sunset, when every window-pane flung back the lustre of a conflagration; and magnificently did it strike upon the eye of the liegemen as they sat at their doors, at that hour, gazing upon the glorious river and its tranquil banks. Nor less pleasant was it to the inmates of the baronial mansion to look back upon the fair village-city, studding the level plain with its scattered dwellings which seemed to sleep upon the grassy and shaded sward.

A garden occupied the space between the proprietary residence and the fort, and through it a pathway led to a dry moat which formed one of the defences of the stronghold, into which admission was obtained from this quarter by a narrow bridge and postern gate. A palisade of sharp pickets fringed the outer and inner slopes of the ditch,—or, to speak more technically, guarded the scarp and counter-scarp. The fort itself sat like a square bonnet on the brow of the headland. Its ramparts of earth were faced outwardly by heavy frame-work of hewn logs, which, on the side looking askant towards the town, were penetrated by an arched gateway and secured by heavy doors studded thick with nails. This portal opened upon a road which lay along the beach beneath the cliff, all the way to the upper extremity of the town. Several low buildings within, appropriated to barracks and magazines, just peered above the ramparts. A few pieces of brass cannon showed like watch-dogs against the horizon, and, high above all, fluttered the provincial banner bearing the cross of England, and holding the relation of a feather to the squat bonnet which the outline of the work might suggest to one curious to trace resemblances.

The province, it may be surmised, was belligerent at this day. For although the Lords Barons of Baltimore, absolute Proprietaries of Maryland and Avalon, would fain have encouraged a pacific temper, and desired ever to treat with the Indians upon terms of friendly bargain and sale, and in all points of policy manifested an equitable disposition towards the native men of the forest, the province, nevertheless, had its full share of hard blows. There was seldom a period, in this early time, when some Indian quarrel was not coming to a head; and, young as the province was, it had already tasted of rebellion at the hands of Clayborne, and Ingle,—to say nothing of that Fendall who was fain to play Cromwell in the plantation, by turning the burgesses out of their hall, and whose sedition hath still something to do with my story.—However peaceable, therefore, the Lord Proprietary might incline to be, he could not but choose stand by his weapons.

In the view of these and kindred troubles, the freemen of the province had no light service in their obligations of military duty. One of the forms in which this service was exacted, in addition to the occasional requisition, on emergency, of the whole population fit to bear arms, and in addition also to a force of mounted rangers who were constantly engaged in scouring the frontier, was in the maintenance of a regularly paid and trained body of musqueteers who supplied the necessary garrisons for the principal forts. That of St. Mary's, which was the oldest and most redoubtable strong-hold in the province, was furnished with a company of forty men of this class who were, at the date of this tale, under the command of a personage of some note, Captain Jasper Dauntrees, to whom I propose to introduce my reader with something more than the slight commendation of a casual acquaintance.

This worthy had been bred up to the science of arms from early youth, and had seen many varieties of service,—first, in the civil wars in which he took the field with the royal army, a staunch cavalier,—and afterwards, with a more doubtful complexion of loyalty, when he enlisted with Monk in Scotland, and followed his banner to London in the notable exploit of the Restoration. Yielding to the bent of that humour which the times engendered, and in imitation of many a hungry and peace-despising gallant of his day, he repaired to the continent, where, after various fortunes, he found himself in the train of Turenne and hard at loggerheads with the Prince of Orange, in which passage of his life he enjoyed the soldierly gratification of lending a hand to the famous ravage of the Palatinate.

Some few years before I have presented him in these pages he had come over to Maryland, with a party of Flemings, to gather for his old age that harvest of wealth and ease which the common report promised to all who set foot upon the golden shores of the Indies—Maryland, in vulgar belief, being a part of this land of wonders. The captain neither stumbled upon a gold mine, nor picked up an Indian princess with a dowry of diamonds; but he fared scarce worse, in his own estimation, when he found himself, in a pleasant sunny clime, invested with the rank of captain of musqueteers, with a snug shelter in the fort, a reasonably fair and punctual allowance of pay—much better, than had been his lot under former masters,—and a frank welcome at all times into the mansion of the Lord Proprietary. Add to these the delights more congenial to the training of his past life, a few wet companions, namely, to help him through an evening potation, and no despicable choice of wines and other comforts at the Crow and Archer, where the Captain with due alacrity became a domesticated and privileged guest, and it may still better be comprehended how little he was likely to repine at his fortune.

His figure had, in youth, been evidently remarked for strength and symmetry—but age and varied service, combined with habits of irregular indulgence, had communicated to it a bluff and corpulent dimension. His port nevertheless was erect, and his step as firm as in his days of lustihood. His eye still sparkled with rays but little quenched by time, although unseasonable vigils sometimes rendered it bloodshotten. A thick neck and rosy complexion betokened a hale constitution; and the ripple of a deep and constantly welling humour, that played upon his strongly marked features, expressed in characters that could not be misread, that love of companionship which had been, perhaps, the most frequent shoal upon which his hopes in life had been stranded. His crown was bald and encircled by a fair supply of crisp, curly and silvery hair, whilst a thick grey moustache gave a martial and veteran air to his visnomy.

His dress served to set off his figure to the best advantage. It consisted of the doublet and ruff, short cloak and trunk hose, the parti-coloured stocking and capacious boot proper to the old English costume which, about the period of the Restoration, began to give way to the cumbrous foppery of the last century. This costume was still retained by many in the province, and belonged to the military equipment of the garrison of St. Mary's, where it was fashioned of light green cloth garnished with yellow lace.

Arrayed in this guise, Captain Dauntrees had some excuse for a small share of vanity on the score of having worn well up to a green old age; and it was manifest that he sought to improve this impression by the debonair freedom with which he wore a drab beaver, with its broad flap looped up on one side, leaving his ample brow bared to wind and weather.

This combination of the martinet and free companion exhibited in the dress of the Captain, was a pretty intelligible index to his character, which disclosed a compound, not unfrequent in the civil wars of that period, of the precisian and ruffler,—the cavalier and economist. In the affairs of life,—a phrase which, in regard to him, meant such matters principally and before all others, as related to his own comfort—he was worldly-wise, sagaciously provident, as an old soldier, of whatever advantages his condition might casually supply; in words, he was, indifferently, according to the occasion, a moralist or hot-brained reveller—sometimes affecting the courtier along with the martialist, and mixing up the saws of peaceful thrift with the patter of the campaigns.

As the occasions of my story may enable me to illustrate some of these points in the character of the worthy Captain, I will not forestall the opinion of my readers, regarding him, by further remark,—preferring that he should speak for himself, rather than leave his merits to be certified by so unpractised an adept, as I confess myself to be, in unriddling the secret properties of a person so deserving to be known.

CHAPTER III

"In every creed,"
'Tis on all hands agreed,"
And plainly confest,"
When the weather is hot,"
That we stick to the pot"
And drink of the best."

Old Song.

"Of all seasons of the year, autumn is the most voluptuous, and October the loveliest of months. Then may a man sit at his door—in the sun if he choose, for he will not find it too hot—or in the shade, if it liketh him, for neither will he find this too cool, and there hold converse with his own meditations: or he may ride or walk, dance or sing, for in this October time a man hath heart for any pastime, so rich is the air, and such pleasant imaginations doth it engender. And if he be poetical, therein will he be greatly favoured; for surely never nature puts on such gaudy attire, on earth or sky, as she wears in our October. The morning haze, which the hoarfrost flings up to meet the sun, hangs across the landscape as if made on purpose to enchant the painter; and the evening sunset lights up the heavens with a glory that shall put that painter—even Claude or Salvator—to shame at the inadequacy of his art. And then the woods!—what pallet hath colours for the forest? Of all the months of the year, commend me to October!"

Some such rhapsody as this was running through the thoughts, and breaking forth in slight mutterings from the lips of the Captain of Musqueteers, on an afternoon in this much lauded month of October, in the year I have alluded to in a former chapter, as he sate in front of his quarters in the fort. A small table was displayed upon the pavement, supplied with a flagon, pipes, and drinking cups. The Captain's solid bulk was deposited in a broad arm-chair, close by the table. His sword and cloak lay upon a bench at the door, and a light breeze flickered amongst his short and hoary locks, where they escaped from the cover of a cloth bonnet which he had now substituted for his beaver. A sentinel stood on post at the gate, towards which the Captain, as he slowly quaffed a cup, ever and anon turned an expectant eye. Once or twice he rose from his seat and strode backward and forward across the parade, then visited the rampart, which afforded him a view of the road leading from the town, and finally resumed his seat and renewed his solitary and slow potation.

When the sun had sunk halfway down the flag-staff, the Captain's wishes were crowned by the arrival of a brace of visiters.

The first of these was Garret Weasel, the publican, a thin, small man, in a suit of gray; of a timid carriage and slender voice. He might have been observed for a restless, undefinable eye which seemed to possess the habitual circumspection of a tapster to see the need of a customer; and this expression was sustained by a rabbit-like celerity of motion which raised the opinion of his timidity. There was an air of assentation and reverence in his demeanour, which, perhaps, grew out of the domestic discipline of his spouse, a buxom dame with the heart of a lioness. She had trained Master Garret to her hand, where he might have worn out his days in implicit obedience, had it not luckily fallen out for him, that Captain Dauntrees had settled himself down in this corner of the New World. The Captain being a regular trafficker in the commodities of the Crow and Archer, and no whit over-awed by the supremacy of mine hostess, soon set himself about seducing her worse-half from his allegiance, so far as was necessary, at least, to satisfy his own cravings for company at the fort. He therefore freely made himself the scapegoat of Garret's delinquencies, confiding in the wheedling power of his tongue, to pacify the dame. With all the tapster's humility and meekness, he still followed the Captain through his irregularities with the adhesiveness and submission of a dog—carousing on occasion like a man of stouter mould, and imitating the reveller-tone of his companion with an ambitious though not always successful zeal. He did not naturally lack merriment; but it was not of the boisterous stamp: there was, at his worst outbreak, a glimmering of deference and respect, rising up to a rickety laugh, and a song sometimes, yet without violent clamour; and the salt tears were often wrung from his eyes by the pent-up laughter which his vocation and his subordinate temper had taught him it was unseemly to discharge in a volley.

His companion was a tall, sinewy, and grave person, habited in the guise of a forester—a cap, namely, of undressed deer skin, a buff jerkin, guarded by a broad belt and buckle at the waist, and leggings of brown leather. This was a Fleming, named Arnold de la Grange, who belonged to the corps of wood rangers in the service of the Lord Proprietary. He had arrived in the province in the time of Lord Cecilius, many years before, and had shared much of the toil of the early settlement. His weather-beaten and gaunt form, tawny cheek, and grizzled hair, bespoke a man inured to the hard service of a frontier life, whilst his erect port and firm step, evinced that natural gracefulness which belongs to men trained to the self-dependence necessary to breast the ever-surrounding perils of such a service. He was a man of few words, and these were delivered in a Low Dutch accent, which his long intercourse with the English had failed to correct. When his service on his range was intermitted, Arnold found quarters amongst the retainers of the Proprietary mansion, and the Proprietary himself manifested towards the forester that degree of trust, and even affection, which resulted from a high sense of his fidelity and conduct, and which gave him a position of more privilege than was enjoyed by the other dependents of the establishment. Being, at these intervals, an idler, he was looked upon with favour by the Captain of the fort, who was not slow to profit by the society of such a veteran in the long watches of a dull afternoon. By a customary consequence, Arnold was no less esteemed by the publican.

A bluff greeting and short ceremony placed the visiters at the table, and each, upon a mute signal from the host, appropriated his cup and pipe.

"You are never a true man, Garret Weasel," said the Captain, "to dally so long behind your appointment; and such an appointment, too! state matters would be trifles to it. The round dozen which you lost to me on Dame Dorothy's head gear—a blessing on it!—you did yourself so order it, was to be broached at three of the clock; and now, by my troth, it is something past four. There is culpable laches in it. Idleness is the canker of the spirit, but occupation is the lard of the body, as I may affirm in my own person. Mistress Dorothy, I suspect, has this tardy coming to answer for. I doubt the brow of our brave dame hath been cloudy this afternoon. How is it, Arnold? bachelor, and Dutchman to boot, you will speak without fear."

"The woman," replied Arnold, in a broken English accent, which I do not attempt to convey in syllables, "had her suspicions."

"Hold ye, Captain Dauntrees," eagerly interrupted the innkeeper, drawing up his chair to the table—for he had seated himself a full arms-length off, in awkward deference to his host; "and hold ye, Master Arnold! my wife rules not me, as some evil-minded jesters report: no, in faith! We were much beset to-day. In sooth I could not come sooner. Customers, you know, Captain, better than most men, customers must be answered, and will be answered, when we poor servants go athirst. We were thronged to-day; was it not so, Arnold?"

"That is true," replied the forester; "the wife had her hands full as well as Garret himself. There were traders in the port, to-day, from the Bay Shore and the Isle of Kent, and some from the country back, to hear whether the brigantine had arrived. They had got some story that Cocklescraft should be here."

"I see it," said Dauntrees; "that fellow, Cocklescraft, hath a trick of warning his friends. He never comes into port but there be strange rumours of him ahead; it seems to be told by the pricking of thumbs. St. Mary's is not the first harbour where he drops his anchor, nor Anthony Warden the first to docket his cargo. You understand me."

"You have a bold mind, Captain," said the publican; "you men of the wars speak your thoughts."

"You are none the losers by Master Cocklescraft," interposed Arnold, drily.

"My wife pays honestly for the liquors," said Weasel, as his eye glanced timorously from one to the other of his comrades; "I take no heed of the accounts."

"But the head gear, Garret," rejoined Dauntrees, laughing; "you pay for that, though the mercer saw my coin for it. Twelve bottles of Canary were a good return on that venture. The bauble sits lightly on the head of the dame, and it is but fair that the winnings should rise as lightly into ours. But for Cocklescraft, we should lack these means to be merry. The customs are at a discount on a dark night. Well, be it so. What point of duty calls on us to baulk the skipper in his trade? We are of the land, not of the water; consumers, on the disbursing side of the account, not of the gathering in. The revenue hath its proper friends, and we should neither meddle nor make. Worthy Garret Weasel has good report in the province for the reasonableness of his wines—and long may he deserve that commendation!"

"I thank heaven that I strive to merit the good will of the freemen," interrupted the innkeeper.

"And he is something given to brag of his wines. Faith, and with reason! Spain and Portugal, the Garonne and the Rhine, are his tributaries. Garret, we know the meridian of your El Dorado."

"Nay, nay, Master Captain—your worship is merry; I beseech you——"

"Never mind your beseeching, my modest friend. You scarce do yourself justice. You have his Lordship's license paid for in good round ducatoons—and that's the fee of a clear conscience. So let the trade thrive! The exchequer is not a baby to be in swaddling bands, unable to feed itself. No, it has the eagle's claw, and wants no help from thee, thou forlorn tapster! Make thine honest penny, Garret; all thirsty fellows will stand by thee."

"I would be thought orderly, Master Dauntrees."

"Thou art so computed—to a fault. You would have been so reckoned in Lord Cecil's time; and matters are less straitened now-a-days. Lord Charles gives more play to good living than his father allowed of. You remember his Lordship's father set his face against wines and strong waters."

"He did, gentlemen," said Weasel, squaring himself in his seat with animation. "Heaven forbid I should speak but as becomes me of the honourable Lord Cecil's memory, or of his honourable son! but to my cost, I know that his Lordship's father was no friend to evil courses, or sottish behaviour, or drinking, unless it was in moderation, mark you. But, with humility, I protest the law is something hard on us poor ordinary keepers: for you shall understand, Arnold Grange, that at a sale by outcry, if there should lack wherewithal to pay the debts of the debtor, the publican and vintner are shut out, seeing that the score for wines and strong waters is the last to be paid."

"And good law it is, let me tell you Garret Weasel! Good and wholesome: wisely laid down by the burgesses, and wisely maintained by his Lordship. You rail without cause. Sober habits must be engendered:—your health, comrades! Then it behooves you publicans to be nice in your custom. We will none of your lurdans that can not pay scot and lot—your runagates that fall under the statute of outcry. Let them drink of the clear brook! There is wisdom and virtue in the law. Is it not so, Arnold?"

"It preaches well," replied the forester, as he sent forth a volume of smoke from his lips.

"Another flask, and we will drink to his Lordship," said Dauntrees, who now left the table and returned with the fourth bottle. "Fill up, friends; the evening wears apace. Here's to his Lordship, and his Lordship's ancestors of ever noble and happy memory!"

As Dauntrees smacked his lip upon emptying his cup, he flung himself back in his chair, and in a thoughtful tone ejaculated: "The good Lord Charles has had a heavy time of it since his return from England; these church brawlers would lay gunpowder under our hearth-stones. And then the death of young Lord Cecil, whilst his father was abroad, too; it was a heavy blow. My lady hath never held up her head since."

A pause succeeded to this grave reflection, during which the trio smoked their pipes in silence, which was at length broken by an attenuated sigh from the publican, as he exclaimed, "Well-a-day! the great have their troubles as well as the rest of us. It is my opinion that Heaven will have its will, Captain; that's my poor judgment." And having thus disburdened himself of this weighty sentiment—the weight of it being increased, perhaps, by the pressure of his previous potations—he drained the heel tap, which stood in his glass, and half whispered, when he had done, "That's as good a drop of Canary as ever grew within the horizon of the Peak of Teneriffe."

"Through the good will of friend Cocklescraft," interrupted Dauntrees, suddenly resuming his former gaiety.

"Pray you, Captain Dauntrees," said the publican, with a hurried concern, "think what hurt thy jest may bring upon me. Arnold knows not your merry humour, and may believe, from your speech, that I am not reputable."

"Pish, man; bridle thy foolish tongue! Did I not see the very cask on't at Trencher Rob's? Did I not mark how your sallow cheek took on an ashen complexion, when his Lordship's Secretary, a fortnight since, suddenly showed himself amongst the cedars upon the bank that overlooks your door, when your ill luck would have you to be rolling the cask in open day into thy cellar. The secretary was in a bookish mood, and saw thee not—or, peradventure, was kind, and would not heed."

To this direct testimony, Weasel could only reply by a faint-hearted and involuntary smile which surrendered the point, and left him in a state of silly confusion.

"Never droop in thy courage, worthy Weasel," exclaimed the Captain; "thou art as honest as thy betters; and, to my mind, the wine hath a better smack from its overland journey from St. Jerome's when there was no sun to heat it."

"The secretary," said the innkeeper, anxious to give the conversation another direction, "is a worshipful youth, and a modest, and grows in favour with the townspeople."

"Ay, and is much beloved by his Lordship," added the Captain.

"And comes, I warrant me, of gentle kind, though I have not heard aught of his country or friends. Dorothy, my wife, says that the women almost swear by him, for his quiet behaviour and pretty words—and they have eyes, Captain Dauntrees, for excellence which we have not."

"There is a cloud upon his birth," said Dauntrees, "and a sorrowful tale touching his nurture. I had it from Burton, the master of the ship who brought him with my Lord to the province."

"Indeed, Captain Dauntrees! you were ever quick to pick up knowledge. You have a full ear and a good memory."

"Drink, drink, comrades!" said the Captain. "We should not go dry because the secretary hath had mishaps. If it please you, I will tell the story, though I will not vouch for the truth of what I have only at second hand."

After the listeners had adjusted themselves in their chairs, Dauntrees proceeded.

"There was, in Yorkshire, a Major William Weatherby, who fought against the Parliament—I did not know him, for I was but a stripling at the time—who, when King Charles was beheaded, went over and took service with the States General, and at Arnheim married a lady of the name of Verheyden. Getting tired of the wars, he came back to England with his wife, where they lived together five or six years without children. The story goes that he was a man of fierce and crooked temper; choleric, and unreasonable in his quarrel; and for jealousy, no devil ever equalled him in that amiable virtue. It was said, too, that his living was riotous and unthrifty, which is, in part, the customary sin of soldiership.—I am frank with you, masters."

"You are a good judge, Captain; you have had experience," said the publican.

"There was a man of some mark in the country where this Weatherby lived, a Sir George Alwin, who, taking pity on the unhappy lady, did her sundry acts of kindness—harmless acts, people say; such as you or I, neighbours, would be moved to do for a distressed female; but the lady was of rare beauty, and the husband full of foul fancies.

"About this time, it was unlucky that nature wrought a change, and the lady grew lusty for the first time in six years marriage. To make the story short, Weatherby was free with his dagger, and in the street, at Doncaster, in the midst of a public show, he stabbed Alwin to the heart."

The wood ranger silently shook his head, and the publican opened his watery eyes in astonishment.

"By the aid of a fleet horse and private enemies of the murdered man, Weatherby escaped out of the kingdom, and was never afterwards heard of."

"And died like a dog, I s'pose," said Arnold de la Grange.

"Likely enough," replied Dauntrees.

"The poor lady was struck down with the horror of the deed, and had nearly gone to her grave. But Heaven was kind, and she survived it, and was relieved of her burden in the birth of a son. For some years afterwards, by the bounty of friends, but with many a struggle—for her means were scanty—she made shift to dwell in England. At last she returned to Holland, where she found a resting place in her native earth, having lived long enough to see her son, a well grown lad, safely taken in charge by her brother, a merchant of Antwerp. The parents were both attached to our Church of Rome, and the son was sent by his uncle to the Jesuit school of his own city. Misfortune overtook the merchant, and he died before the nephew had reached his fourteenth year. But the good priests of Antwerp tended the lad with the care of parents, and would have reared him as a servant of the altar. When our Lord Baltimore was in the Netherlands, three years ago, he found Albert Verheyden, (the youth has ever borne his mother's name,) in the Seminary. His Lordship took a liking to him and brought him into his own service. Master Albert was then but eighteen. There is the whole story. It is as dry as a muscat raisin. It sticks in the throat, masters,—so moisten, moisten!"

"It is a marvellous touching story," said the innkeeper, as he swallowed at a draught a full goblet.

"The hot hand and the cold steel," said Arnold, thoughtfully, "hold too much acquaintance in these times. Master Albert is an honest youth, and a good youth, and a brave follower too, of hawk or hound, Captain Dauntrees."

"Then there is good reason for a cup to the secretary," said the Captain, filling again. "The world hath many arguments for a thirsty man. The blight of the year fall upon this sadness! Let us change our discourse—I would carouse a little, friends: It is salutary to laugh. Thanks to my patron, I am a bachelor! So drink, Master Arnold, mein sauff bruder, as we used to say on the Rhine."

"Ich trinck, euch zu," was the reply of the forester, as he answered the challenge with a sparkling eye, and a face lit up with smiles; "a good lad, an excellent lad, though he come of a hot-brained father!"

The wine began to show itself upon the revellers; for by this time they had nearly got through half of the complement of the wager. The effect of this potation upon the Captain was to give him a more flushed brow, and a moister eye, and to administer somewhat to the volubility of his tongue. It had wrought no further harm, for Dauntrees was bottle-proof. Upon the forester it was equally harmless, rather enhancing than dissipating his saturnine steadfastness of demeanour. He was, perchance, somewhat more precise and thoughtful. Garret Weasel, of the three, was the only weak vessel. With every cup of the last half hour he grew more supple.

"Ads heartlikens!" he exclaimed, "but this wine doth tingle, Captain Dauntrees. Here is a fig for my wife Dorothy! Come and go as you list—none of your fetch and carry! that's what the world is coming to, amongst us married cattle!"

"Thou art a valorous tapster," said the Captain.

"I am the man to stand by his friend, Captain mine; and I am thy friend, Captain—Papist or Roman though they call thee!"

"A man for need, Garret!" said Dauntrees, patting him on the head; "a dozen flasks or so, when a friend wants them, come without the asking."

"And I pay my wagers, I warrant, Captain, like a true comrade."

"Like a prince, Garret, who does not stop to count the score, but makes sure of the total by throwing in a handful over."

"I am no puritan, Master Dauntrees, I tell thee."

"Thou hast the port of a cavalier, good Weasel. Thou wouldst have done deadly havoc amongst the round-heads, if they but took thee in the fact of discharging a wager. Thou wert scarce in debt, after this fashion, at Worcester, my valiant drawer. Thy evil destiny kept thee empty on that day."

"Ha, ha, ha! a shrewd memory for a stale jest, Captain Dauntrees. The world is slanderous, though I care little for it. You said you would be merry; shall we not have a song? Come, troll us a catch, Captain."

"I am of thy humour, old madcap; I'll wag it with thee bravely," replied Dauntrees, as he struck up a brisk drinking-bout glee of that day, in which he was followed by the treble voice of the publican, who at the same time rose from his seat and accompanied the music with some unsteady gyrations in the manner of a dance upon the gravel.

"From too much keeping an evil decorum,
From the manifold treason parliamentorum,
From Oliver Cromwell, dux omnium malorum,
Libera nos, Libera nos."

Whilst Dauntrees and his gossips were thus occupied in their carouse, they were interrupted by the unexpected arrival of two well known persons, who had approached by the path of the postern gate.

The elder of the two was a youth just on the verge of manhood. His person was slender, well proportioned, and rather over the common height. His face, distinguished by a decided outline of beauty, wore a thoughtful expression, which was scarcely overcome by the flash of a black and brilliant eye. A complexion pale and even feminine, betokened studious habits. His dress, remarkable for its neatness, denoted a becoming pride of appearance in the wearer. It told of the Low Countries. A well-fitted doublet and hose, of a grave colour, were partially concealed by a short camlet cloak of Vandyke brown. A black cap and feather, a profusion of dark hair hanging in curls towards the shoulders, and a falling band or collar of lace, left it unquestionable that the individual I have sketched was of gentle nurture, and associated with persons of rank. This was further manifested in the gay and somewhat gaudy apparel of his companion,—a lad of fourteen, who walked beside him in the profusely decorated costume of a young noble of that ambitious era, when the thoughtless and merry monarch of England, instead of giving himself to the cares of government, was busy to invent extravagancies of dress. The lad was handsome, though his features wore the impress of feeble health. He now bore in his hand a bow and sheaf of arrows.

The visiters had taken our revellers at unawares, and had advanced within a few feet before they were observed. The back of the publican was turned to them, and he was now in mid career of his dance, throwing up his elbows, tossing his head, and treading daintily upon the earth, as he sang the burden,

"Libera nos, libera nos."

"You give care a holiday, Captain Dauntrees," said the elder youth, with a slightly perceptible foreign accent.

Dauntrees started abruptly from his seat, at this accost, smiled with a reddened brow, and made a low obeisance. The cessation of the song left Garret Weasel what a mariner would term "high and dry," for like a bark floated upon a beach and suddenly bereft of its element, he remained fixed in the attitude at which the music deserted him,—one foot raised, an arm extended, and his face turned inquiringly over his shoulder. His amazement upon discovering the cause of this interruption, brought about a sudden and ludicrous affectation of sobriety; in an instant his port was changed into one of deference, although somewhat awkwardly overcharged with what was intended to represent gravity and decorum.

Arnold de la Grange rose from his chair and stood erect, firm and silent.

"Hail, Master Albert Verheyden, and Master Benedict Leonard: God save you both!" said Dauntrees.

"I say amen to that, and God save his lordship, besides!" ejaculated the publican with a drunken formality of utterance.

"I would not disturb your merriment, friends," said the secretary, "but his lordship bade me summon Captain Dauntrees to the hall. You, Arnold de la Grange, will be pleased to accompany the Captain."

Arnold bowed his head, and the visiters retired by the great gate of the fort. In a moment young Benedict Leonard came running back, and addressed the forester—

"Master Arnold, I would have a new bow-string—this is worn; and my bird-bolts want feathering: shall I leave them with you, good Arnold?" And without waiting an answer, he thrust the bow and arrows into the smiling wood-ranger's hand, and bounded away again through the gate.

Dauntrees flung his sword-belt across his shoulder, put on his cloak, delayed a moment to secure the remaining flasks of wine, and then beckoned to the ranger to follow him.

"Stop," cried Weasel, with an officious zeal to make himself useful; "your belt is awry: it is not comely to be seen by his lordship in this slovenly array."

The belt was set right, and the two directed their steps towards the postern, and thence to the mansion. The publican tarried only until his companions were out of sight, when, curious to know the object of the errand, and careful to avoid the appearance of intrusion, he followed upon the same path, at a respectful distance,—stepping wisely, as a drunken man is wont, and full of the opinion that his sobriety was above all suspicion.

CHAPTER IV

> Oft as the peasant wight impelled
> To these untrodden paths had been,
> As oft he, horror struck, beheld
> Things of unearthly shape and mien.
>
> Glengonar's Wassail.

The day was drawing near to a close, and the Proprietary thoughtfully paced the hall. The wainscoted walls around him were hung with costly paintings, mingled, not untastefully, with Indian war clubs, shields, bows and arrows, and other trophies won from the savage. There were also the ponderous antlers of the elk and the horns of the buck sustaining draperies of the skins of beasts of prey. Musquets, cutlasses and partisans were bestowed on brackets ready for use in case of sudden invasion from that race of wild men whose stealthy incursions in times past had taught this policy of preparation. The level rays of the setting sun, striking through the broad open door, flung a mellow radiance over the hall, giving a rich picture-like tone to its sylvan furniture.

Lord Baltimore, at the period when I have introduced him, might have been verging upon fifty. He was of a delicate and slender stature, with a grave and dignified countenance. His manners were sedate and graceful, and distinguished by that gentleness which is characteristic of an educated mind when chastened by affliction. He had been schooled to this gentleness both by domestic and public griefs. The loss of a favourite son, about two years before, had thrown a shadow upon his spirit, and a succession of unruly political irritations in the province served to prevent the return of that buoyancy of heart which is indifferently slow to come back at middle age, even when solicited by health, fortune, friends, and all the other incitements which, in younger men, are wont to lift up a wounded spirit out of the depths of a casual sorrow.

Charles Calvert had come to the province in 1662, and from that date, until the death of his father, thirteen years afterwards, administered the government in the capacity of Lieutenant-General. Upon his accession to the proprietary rights, he found himself compelled by the intrigues of a faction to visit London, where he was detained nearly four years,—having left Lady Baltimore, with a young family of children, behind him, under the care of his uncle Philip Calvert, the chancellor of the province. He had now, within little more than a twelvemonth, returned to his domestic roof, to mingle his sorrows with those of his wife for the death of his eldest son, Cecilius, who had sunk into the tomb during his absence.

The public cares of his government left him scant leisure to dwell upon his personal afflictions. The province was surrounded by powerful tribes of Indians who watched the white settlers with an eager hostility, and seized every occasion to molest them by secret inroad, and often by open assault. A perpetual war of petty reprisals, prevailed upon the frontier, and even sometimes invaded the heart of the province.

A still more vexatious annoyance existed in the party divisions of the inhabitants—divisions unluckily resting on religious distinctions—the most fierce of all dissensions. Ever since the Restoration, the jealousy of the Protestant subjects of the crown against the adherents of the church of Rome had been growing into a sentiment that finally broke forth into the most flagrant persecution. In the province, the Protestants during the last twenty years had greatly increased in number, and at the date of this narrative constituted already the larger mass of the population. They murmured against the dominion of the Proprietary as one adverse to the welfare of the English church; and intrigues were set on foot to obtain the establishment of that church in the province through the interest of the ministry in England. Letters were written by some of the more ambitious clergy of Maryland to the Archbishop of Canterbury to invoke his aid in the enterprise. The government of Lord Baltimore was traduced in these representations, and every disorder attributed to the ascendancy of the Papists. It was even affirmed that the Proprietary and his uncle the Chancellor, had instigated the Indians to ravage the plantations of the Protestant settlers, and to murder their families. Chiefly, to counteract these intrigues, Lord Baltimore had visited the court at London. Cecilius Calvert, the founder of the province, with a liberality as wise as it was unprecedented, had erected his government upon a basis of perfect religious freedom. He did this at a time when he might have incorporated his own faith with the political character of the colony, and maintained it, by a course of legislation, which would, perhaps, even up to the present day, have rendered Maryland the chosen abode of those who now acknowledge the founder's creed. His views, however, were more expansive. It was his design to furnish in Maryland a refuge not only to the weary and persecuted votaries of his own sect, but an asylum to all who might wish for shelter in a land where opinion should be free and conscience undisturbed. Whilst this plant of toleration was yet young, it grew with a healthful luxuriance; but the popular leaders, who are not always as truly and consistently attached to enlightened freedom as we might be led to believe from their boasting, and who incessantly aim to obtain power and make it felt, had no sooner acquired strength to battle with the Proprietary than they rooted up the beautiful exotic and gave it to the winds.

Amongst the agitators in this cause was a man of some note in the former history of the province—the famous Josias Fendall, the governor in the time of the Protectorate—now in a green old age, whose turbulent temper, and wily propensity to mischief had lost none of their edge with the approach of grey hairs. This individual had stimulated some of the hot spirits of the province into open rebellion against the life of the Proprietary and his uncle. His chief associate was John Coode, a coarse but shrewd leader of a faction, who, with the worst inclinations against the Proprietary had the wit to avoid the penalties of the law, and to maintain himself in a popular position as a member of the house of Burgesses. Fendall, a few months before this era, had been arrested with several followers, upon strong proofs of conspiracy, and was now a close prisoner in the gaol.

Such is a brief but necessary view of the state of affairs on the date, at which I have presented the Lord Proprietary to my reader. The matter now in hand with the captain of the fort had reference to troubles of inferior note to those which I have just recounted.

When Lord Baltimore descried Captain Dauntrees and the ranger approaching the mansion from the direction of the fort, he advanced beyond the threshold to meet them. In a moment they stood unbonneted before him.

"God save you, good friends!" was his salutation—"Captain Dauntrees and worthy Arnold, welcome!—Cover,"—he added in a tone of familiar kindness,—"put on your hats; these evening airs sometimes distill an ague upon a bare head."

A rugged smile played upon the features of the old forester as he resumed his shaggy cap, and said, "Lord Charles is good; but he does not remember that the head of an old ranger gets his blossoms like the dog-wood,—in the wind and the rain:—the dew sprinkles upon it the same as upon a stone."

"Old friend," replied the Proprietary,—"that grizzly head has taken many a sprinkling in the service of my father and myself: it is worthy of a better bonnet, and thou shalt have one, Arnold—the best thou canst find in the town. Choose for yourself, and Master Verheyden shall look to the cost of it."

The Fleming modestly bowed, as he replied with that peculiar foreign gesture and accent, neither of which may be described,—"Lord Charles is good.—He is the son of his father, Lord Cecil,—Heaven bless his memory!"

"Master Verheyden, bade me attend your lordship," said Dauntrees; "and to bring Arnold de la Grange with me."

"I have matter for your vigilance, Captain," replied the Proprietary. "Walk with me in the garden—we will talk over our business in the open air."

When they had strolled some distance, Lord Baltimore proceeded—"There are strange tales afloat touching certain mysterious doings in a house at St. Jerome's: the old wives will have it that it is inhabited by goblins and mischievous spirits—and, in truth, wiser people than old women are foolish enough to hold it in dread. Father Pierre tells me he can scarcely check this terror."

"Your Lordship means the fisherman's house on the beach at St. Jerome's," said the Captain. "The country is full of stories concerning it, and it has long had an ill fame. I know the house: the gossips call it The Wizard's Chapel. It stands hard by the hut of The Cripple. By my faith,—he who wanders there at nightfall had need of a clear shrift."

"You give credence to these idle tales?"

"No idle tales, an please your Lordship. Some of these marvels have I witnessed with my own eyes. There is a curse of blood upon that roof."

"I pray you speak on," said the Proprietary, earnestly; "there is more in this than I dreamed of."

"Paul Kelpy the fisherman," continued Dauntrees,—"it was before my coming into the province—but the story goes——"

"It was in the Lord Cecil's time—I knowed the fisherman," interrupted Arnold.

"He was a man," said the Captain, "who, as your Lordship may have heard, had a name which caused him to be shunned in his time,—and they are alive now who can tell enough of his wickedness to make one's hair rise on end. He dwelt in this house at St. Jerome's in Clayborne's day, and took part with that freebooter;—went with him, as I have heard, to the Island, and was outlawed."

"Ay, and met the death he deserved—I remember the story," said the Proprietary. "He was foiled in his attempt to get out of the province, and barred himself up in his own house."

"And there he fought like a tiger,—or more like a devil as he was," added the ranger. "They were more than two days, before they could get into his house."

"When his door was forced at last," continued the Captain; "they found him, his wife and child lying in their own blood upon the hearth stone. They were all murdered, people say, by his own hand."

"And that was true!" added Arnold; "I remember how he was buried at the cross road, below the Mattapany Fort, with a stake drove through his body."

"Ever since that time," continued Dauntrees, "they say the house has been without lodgers—of flesh and blood, I mean, my Lord,—for it has become a devil's den, and a busy one."

"What hast thou seen, Captain? You speak as a witness."

"It is not yet six months gone by, my Lord, when I was returning with Clayton, the master of the collector's pinnace, from the Isle of Kent; we stood in, after night, towards the headland of St. Jerome's bay;—it was very dark—and the four windows of the Wizard's Chapel, that looked across the beach, were lighted up with such a light as I have never seen from candle or fagot. And there were antic figures passing the blaze that seemed deep in some hellish carouse. We kept our course, until we got almost close aboard,—when suddenly all grew dark. There came, at that moment, a gust of wind such as the master said he never knew to sweep in daylight across the Chesapeake. It struck us in our teeth, and we were glad to get out again upon the broad water. It would seem to infer that the Evil One had service rendered there, which it would be sinful to look upon. In my poor judgment it is matter for the church, rather than for the hand of the law."

"You are not a man, Captain Dauntrees, to be lightly moved by fantasies," said the Proprietary, gravely; "you have good repute for sense and courage. I would have you weigh well what you report."

"Surely, my Lord, Clayton is as stout a man in heart as any in the province: and yet he could scarcely hold his helm for fear."

"Why was I not told of this?"

"Your Lordship's favour," replied Dauntrees, shaking his head; "neither the master, the seamen nor myself would hazard ill will by moving in the matter. There is malice in these spirits, my Lord, which will not brook meddling in their doings: we waited until we might be questioned by those who had right to our answer. The blessed martyrs shield me! I am pledged to fight your Lordship's bodily foes:—the good priests of our holy patron St. Ignatius were better soldiers for this warfare."

The Proprietary remained for some moments silent: at last, turning to the ranger, he inquired—"What dost thou know of this house, Arnold?"

"Well, Lord Charles," replied the veteran, "I was not born to be much afeard of goblins or witches.—In my rangings I have more than once come in the way of these wicked spirits; and then I have found that a clean breast and a stout heart, with the help of an Ave Mary and a Paternoster was more than a match for all their howlings. But the fisherman's house—oh, my good Lord Charles," he added with a portentous shrug, "has dwellers in it that it is best not to trouble. When Sergeant Travers and myself were ranging across by St. Jerome's, at that time when Tiquassino's men were thought to be a thieving,—last Hallowmass, if I remember,—we shot a doe towards night, and set down in the woods, waiting to dress our meat for a supper, which kept us late, before we mounted our horses again. But we had some aqua vitæ, and didn't much care for hours. So it was midnight, with no light but the stars to show us our way. It happened that we rode not far from the Wizard's Chapel, which put us to telling stories to each other about Paul Kelpy and the ghosts that people said haunted his house."

"The aqua vitæ made you talkative as well as valiant, Arnold," interrupted the Proprietary.

"I will not say that," replied the ranger; "but something put it into our heads to go down the bank and ride round the chapel. At first all was as quiet as if it had been our church here of St. Mary's—except that our horses snorted and reared with fright at something we could not see. The wind was blowing, and the waves were beating on the shore,—and suddenly we began to grow cold; and then, all at once, there came a rumbling noise inside of the house like the rolling of a hogshead full of pebbles, and afterwards little flashes of light through the windows, and the sergeant said he heard clanking chains and groans:—it isn't worth while to hide it from your lordship, but the sergeant ran away like a coward, and I followed him like another, Lord Charles.—Since that night I have not been near the Black house.—We have an old saying in my country—'een gebrande kat vreest het koude water'—the scalded cat keeps clear of cold water—ha, I mind the proverb."

"It is not long ago," said Dauntrees, "perhaps not above two years,—when, they say, the old sun-dried timber of the building turned suddenly black. It was the work of a single night—your Lordship shall find it so now."

"I can witness the truth of it," said Arnold—"the house was never black until that night, and now it looks as if it was scorched with lightning from roof to ground sill. And yet, lightning could never leave it so black without burning it to the ground."

"There is some trickery in this," said the Proprietary. "It may scarce be accounted for on any pretence of witchcraft, or sorcery, although I know there are malignant influences at work in the province which find motive enough to do all the harm they can. Has Fendall, or any of his confederates had commerce with this house, Captain Dauntrees? Can you suspect such intercourse?"

"Assuredly not, my Lord," replied the Captain, "for Marshall, who is the most insolent of that faction, hath, to my personal knowledge, the greatest dread of the chapel of all other men I have seen. Besides, these terrors have flourished in the winter-night tales of the neighbourhood, ever since the death of Kelpy, and long before the Fendalls grew so pestilent in the province."

"It is the blood of the fisherman, my good Lord, and of his wife and children that stains the floor," said Arnold; "it is that blood which brings the evil spirits together about the old hearth. Twice every day the blood-spots upon the floor freshen and grow strong, as the tide comes to flood;—at the ebb they may be hardly seen."

"You have witnessed this yourself, Arnold?"

"At the ebb, Lord Charles. I did not stay for the change of tide. When I saw the spots it was as much as we could do to make them out.—But at the flood every body says they are plain."

"It is a weighty matter, a very weighty matter, an it like your Lordship's honour," muttered forth the slim voice of Garret Weasel, who had insinuated himself, by slow approach, into the rear of the company, near enough to hear a part of this conversation, and who now fancied that his interest in the subject would ensure him an unrebuked access to the Proprietary—"and your Lordship hath a worthy care for the fears of the poor people touching the abominations of the Wizard's Chapel."

"What brought thee here, Garret Weasel?" inquired the Proprietary, as he turned suddenly upon the publican and looked him steadfastly in the face—"What wonder hast thou to tell to excuse thy lurking at our heels?"

"Much and manifold, our most noble Lord, touching the rumours," replied the confused innkeeper, with a thick utterance. "And it is the most notable thing about it that Robert Swale—Rob o' the Trencher, as he is commonly called—your Lordship apprehends I mean the Cripple—that Rob lives so near the Wizard's Chapel. There's matter of consideration in that—if your Lordship will weigh it."

"Fie, Master Garret Weasel! Fie on thee! Thou art in thy cups. I grieve to see thee making a beast of thyself. You had a name for sobriety. Look that you lose it not again. Captain Dauntrees if the publican has been your guest this evening, you are scarce free of blame for this."

"He has a shallow head, my Lord, and it is more easily sounded than I guessed. Arnold," said Dauntrees apart—"persuade the innkeeper home."

The ranger took Garret's arm, and expostulating with him as he led him away, dismissed him at the gate with an admonition to bear himself discreetly in the presence of his wife,—a hint which seemed to have a salutary effect, as the landlord was seen shaping his course with an improved carriage towards the town.

"Have you reason to believe, Captain Dauntrees," said the Proprietary, after Weasel had departed; "that the Cripple gives credit to these tales. He lives near this troubled house?"

"Not above a gunshot off, my Lord. He cannot but be witness to these marvels. But he is a man of harsh words, and lives to himself. There is matter in his own life, I should guess, which leaves but little will to censure these doings. To a certainty he has no fear of what may dwell in the Black building.—I have seldom spoken with him."

"Your report and Arnold's," said the Proprietary, "confirm the common rumour. I have heard to-day, that two nights past some such phantoms as you speak of have been seen, and deemed it at first a mere gossip's wonder;—but what you tell gives a graver complexion of truth to these whisperings. Be there demons or jugglers amongst us—and I have reason to suspect both—this matter must be sifted. I would have the inquiry made by men who are not moved by the vulgar love of marvel. This duty shall be yours, friends. Make suitable preparation, Captain, to discharge it at your earliest leisure. I would have you and Arnold, with such discreet friends as you may select, visit this spot at night and observe the doings there. Look that you keep your own counsel:—we have enemies of flesh and blood that may be more dreaded than these phantoms. So, God speed you friends!"

"The man who purges the Black House of the fiend, so please you, my Lord," said Dauntrees, "should possess more odour of sanctity than I doubt will be found under our soldier's jerkins. I shall nevertheless execute your Lordship's orders to the letter."

"Hark you, Captain," said the Proprietary, as his visiters were about to take their leave—"if you have a scruple in this matter and are so inclined, I would have you confer with Father Pierre. Whether this adventure require prayer, or weapon of steel, you shall judge for yourself."

"I shall take it, my Lord, as a point of soldiership," said Dauntrees, "to be dealt with, in soldierly fashion—that is, with round blows if occasion serves. I ask no aid from our good priest. He hath a trick—if I may be so bold as to speak it before your Lordship—which doth not so well sort with my age and bodily health,—a trick, my Lord, of putting one to a fasting penance by way of purification. Our purpose of visiting the Black House would be unseasonably delayed by such a purgation."

"As thou wilt—as thou wilt!" said the Proprietary, laughing; "Father Pierre would have but an idle sinecure, if he had no other calling but to bring thee to thy penitentiary.—Good even, friends,—may the kind saints be with you!"

The Captain and his comrade now turned their steps toward the fort, and the Proprietary retired into the mansion. Here he found the secretary and Benedict Leonard waiting his arrival. They had just returned from the town, whither they had gone after doing their errand to the fort. Albert Verheyden bore a packet secured with silken strings and sealed, which he delivered to the Proprietary.

"Dick Pagan, the courier," he said, "has just come in from James Town in Virginia, whence he set forth but four days ago—he has had a hard ride of it—and brought this pacquet to the sheriff for my Lord. The courier reports that a ship had just arrived from England, and that Sir Henry Chichely the governor gave him this for your Lordship to be delivered without delay."

The Proprietary took the pacquet: "Albert," he said, as he was about to withdraw, "I have promised the old ranger, Arnold de la Grange, a new cap. Look to it:—get him the best that you may find in the town—or, perhaps, it would better content him to have one made express by Cony the leather dresser. Let it be as it may best please the veteran himself, good Albert." With this considerate remembrance of the ranger, Lord Baltimore withdrew into his study.

CHAPTER V

—-deep on his front engraven,
Deliberation sat, and public care.

Milton.

Lend me thy lantern quoth a? Marry I'll see thee hanged first.

Shakspeare.

A small fire blazed on the hearth of the study and mingled its light with that of a silver cresset, which hung from the ceiling above a table furnished with writing materials and strewed over with papers. Here the Proprietary sat intent upon the perusal of the pacquet. Its contents disquieted him; and with increasing solicitude he again and again read over the letters.

At length the secretary was summoned into his presence. "Albert," he said, "the council must be called together to-morrow at noon. The messengers should be despatched to-night; they have a dark road and far to ride. Let them be ready with the least delay."

The secretary bowed and went forth to execute his order.

The letters brought the Proprietary a fresh importation of troubles. That which most disturbed him was from the Board of Trade and Plantations, and spoke authoritatively of the growing displeasure of the ministry at the exclusiveness, as it was termed, of the Proprietary's favours, in the administration of his government, to the Catholic inhabitants of the province; it hinted at the popular and probably well-founded discontent—to use its own phrase—of his Majesty's Protestant subjects against the too liberal indulgence shown to the Papists; repeated stale charges and exploded calumnies against the Proprietary, with an earnestness that showed how sedulously his enemies had taken advantage of the disfavour into which the Church of Rome and its advocates had fallen since the Restoration; and concluded with a peremptory intimation of the royal pleasure that all the offices of the province should be immediately transferred into the hands of the Church of England party.

This was a blow at Lord Baltimore which scarcely took him by surprise. His late visit to England had convinced him that not all the personal partiality of the monarch for his family—and this was rendered conspicuous in more than one act of favour at a time when the Catholic lords were brought under the ban of popular odium—would be able finally to shelter the province from that religious proscription which already was rife in the mother land. He was not, therefore, altogether unprepared to expect this assault. The mandate was especially harsh in reference to the Proprietary, first because it was untrue that he had ever recognised the difference of religious opinion in his appointments, but on the contrary had conferred office indiscriminately in strict and faithful accordance with the fundamental principle of toleration upon which his government was founded; and secondly, because it would bear with pointed injustice upon some of his nearest and most devoted friends—his uncle the chancellor, the whole of his council, and, above all others in whose welfare he took an interest, upon the collector of the port of St. Mary's, Anthony Warden, an old inhabitant of the province, endeared to the Proprietary—and indeed to all his fellow-burgesses—by long friendship and tried fidelity. What rendered it the more grating to the feelings of the Proprietary in this instance, was that the collectorship had already been singled out as a prize to be played for by that faction which had created the late disturbances in the province. It was known that Coode had set his eyes upon this lure, and gloated upon it with the gaze of a serpent. The emoluments of the post were something considerable, and its importance was increased by the influence it was supposed to confer on the incumbent, as a person of weight and consequence in the town.

The first expression of irritation which the perusal of the pacquet brought to the lips of the Proprietary had a reference to the collector. "They would have me," he said, as he rose and strode through the apartment, "discard from my service, the very approved friends with whom in my severest toils, in this wilderness, I have for so many years buffeted side by side, and to whom I am most indebted for support and encouragement amidst the thousand disasters of my enterprise. They would have me turn adrift, without a moment's warning, and even with circumstances of disgrace, that tried pattern of honesty, old Anthony Warden. Virtue, in her best estate, hath but a step-daughter's portion in the division of this world's goods, and often goes begging, when varnished knavery carries a high head and proud heart, and lords it like a very king. By the blessed light! old Anthony shall not budge on my motion. Am I to be schooled in my duty by rapacious malcontents, and to be driven to put away my trustiest friends, to make room for such thirsty leeches and coarse rufflers as John Coode? The argument is, that here, in what my father would have made a peaceful, contented land, planted by him and the brothers of his faith,—with the kindest, best and most endeared supporters of that faith by my side—worthy men, earnest and zealous to do their duty—they and their children true to every christian precept—men who have won a home by valour and patient, wise endurance—they must all be disfranchised, as not trustworthy even for the meanest office, and give their places to brawlers, vapouring bullies and factious stirrers-up of discord—and that too in the name of religion! Oh, this viper of intolerance, how hath it crept in and defiled the garden! One would have thought this world were wide enough to give the baser passions elbow room, without rendering our little secluded nook a theatre for the struggle. Come what may, Anthony Warden shall not lack the collectorship whilst a shred of my prerogative remains untorn!"

In this strain of feeling the Proprietary continued to chafe his spirit, until the necessity of preparing the letters which were to urge the attendance of his council, drew him from his fretful reverie into a calmer tone of mind.

In the servants' hall there was an unusual stir occasioned by the preparations which were in train for the outriding of the messengers whom the secretary had put in requisition for the service of the night. The first of these was Derrick Brown, a man of stout mould though somewhat advanced in years. He held in the establishment what might be termed the double post of master of the mews and keeper of the fox hounds, being principal falconer and huntsman of the household. The second was a short, plump little fellow, bearing the name of John Alward, who was one of the grooms of the stable. These two, now ready booted, belted and spurred, were seated on a bench, discussing a luncheon, with the supplement of a large jack or tankard of brown bastard. Several of the other domestics loitered in the hall, throwing in occasionally a word of advice to the riders, or giving them unsolicited aid in the carnal occupation of bodily reinforcement to which they were devoting themselves with the lusty vigour of practised trenchermen. Leaning against the jamb of the ample fireplace, immediately below a lamp which tipped the prominent points of his grave visage with a sharp light, stood an old Indian, of massive figure and swarthy hue, named Pamesack, or, as he was called in the English translation of the Indian word, The Knife. This personage had been, for some years past, at intervals, a privileged inmate of the Proprietary's family, and was now, though consigned to a portion of the duties of the evening, apparently an unconcerned spectator of the scene around him. He smoked his pipe in silence, or if he spoke, it was seldom more than in the short monosyllable, characteristic of the incommunicative habits of his tribe.

"When I saw Dick Pagan, the James Town courier, coming into town this evening with his leather pouch slung across his shoulder," said the elder of the riders, "I guessed as much as that there would be matter for the council. News from that quarter now-a-days is apt to bring business for their worships. I warrant you the brother of Master Fendall hath been contriving an outcome in Virginia. I heard John Rye, the miller of St. Clements, say last Sunday afternoon, that Samuel Fendall had forty mounted men ready in the forest to do his bidding with broad-sword and carbine. And he would have done it too, if my Lord had not laid him by the heels at unawares. He hath a savage spite against my Lord and the chancellor both."

"But knew ye ever the like before," said John Alward, "that his lordship should be in such haste to see their worships, he must needs have us tramping over the country at midnight? By the virtue of my belt, there must be a hot flavour in the news! It was a post haste letter."

"Tush, copperface! What have you to do with the flavour of the news? The virtue of thy belt, indeed! Precious little virtue is there within its compass, ha, ha! You have little to complain of, John Alward, for a midnight tramp. It is scant twelve miles from this to Mattapany, and thine errand is done. Thou mayst be snoozing on a good truss of hay in Master Sewall's stable before midnight, if you make speed. Think of my ride all the way to Notley Hall,—and round about by the head of the river too—for I doubt if I have any chance to get a cast over the ferry to-night. Simon the boat-keeper is not often sober at this hour: and if he was, a crustier churl—the devil warm his pillow!—doesn't live 'twixt this and the old world. He gets out of his sleep for no man."

"But it is a dark road mine," replied the groom. "A plague upon it! I have no stomach for this bush and brier work, when a man can see the limb of a tree no more than a cobweb."

"A dark road!" exclaimed the master of the kennels, laughing. "A dark road, John! It is a long time, I trow, since there has been a dark road for thy night rides, with that nose shining like a lighted link a half score paces around thee. It was somewhat deadened last September, I allow, when you had the marsh ague, and the doctor fed you for a week on gruel—but it hath waxed lately as bright as ever. I wish I could buckle it to my head-strap until to-morrow morning."

A burst of laughter, at this sally, which rang through the hall, testified the effect of the falconer's wit and brought the groom to his feet.

"'S blood, you grinning fools!" he ejaculated, "haven't you heard Derrick's joke a thousand times before, that you must toss up your scurvy ha-haws at it, as if it was new! He stole it—as the whole hundred knows—from the fat captain, old Dauntrees in the fort there; who would have got it back upon hue and cry, if it had been his own;—but the truth is, the Captain filched it from a play-book, as the surveyor told him in my hearing at Garret Weasel's, where the Captain must needs have it for a laughing matter."

"It is a joke that burns fresh every night," replied Derrick; "a thing to make light of. So, up with the bottom of the pot, boy, and feed it with mother's milk: it will stand thee in stead to-night. Well done, John Alward! I can commend thee for taking a jest as well as another."

"Master Derrick," said the other, "this is not the way to do his Lordship's bidding: if we must go, we should be jogging now. I would I had thy ride to take, instead of my own,—short as you think it."

"Ha, say you that! By the rochet, John, you shall have it, an it please Master Secretary! But upon one condition."

"Upon what condition?"

"That you tell me honestly why you would choose to ride twenty miles to Notley rather than twelve to Mattapany."

"Good Derrick," answered the groom, "it is but as a matter of horsemanship. You have a broader road, and mine is a path much beset with brush-wood. I like not the peril of being unhorsed."

"There is a lie in thy face, John Alward;—the Mattapany road is the broadest and best of the two—is it not so, Pamesack?"

"It is the first that was opened by the white man," replied the Indian; "and more people pass upon it than the other."

"John," said the falconer, "you are a coward. I will not put you to the inventing another lie, but will wager I can tell you at one guess why you would change with me."

"Out with it, Master Derrick!" exclaimed the bystanders.

"Oh, out with it!" repeated John Alward; "I heed not thy gibes."

"You fear the cross road," said the falconer; "you will not pass the fisherman's grave."

"In troth, masters—I must needs own," replied the groom, "that I have qualms. I never was ashamed to tell the truth, and confess that I am so much of a sinner as to feel an honest fear of the devil and his doings. I have known a horse to start and a rider to be flung at the cross road before now:—there are times in the night when both horse and rider may see what it turns one's blood into ice to look at. Nay, I am in earnest, masters:—I jest not."

"Thou hast honestly confessed, like a brave man, that thou art a coward, John Alward; and so it shall be a bargain between us. I will take your message. I fear not Paul Kelpy—he has been down with that stake through his body, ever too fast to walk abroad."

"There's my hand to it," said the groom, "and thanks to boot. I am no coward, Derrick,—but have an infirmity which will not endure to look by night in the lonesome woods, upon a spirit which walks with a great shaft through it. Willy of the Flats saw it, in that fashion, as he went home from the Viewer's feast on the eve of St. Agnes."

"Willy had seen too much of the Viewer's hollands that night," said Derrick; "and they are spirits worth a dozen Paul Kelpys, even if the whole dozen were trussed upon the same stake, like herrings hung up to smoke. In spite of the fisherman and his bolt, I warrant you I pass unchallenged betwixt this and Mattapany."

The secretary, soon after this, entered the hall and confirmed the arrangements which had just been made. He accordingly delivered the letters intended for Colonel Talbot and Nicholas Sewall to the falconer, and that for Mr. Notley, the late lieutenant general of the province, to John Alward. To the Indian was committed the duty of bearing the missions to such members of the council as resided either in the town or within a few miles of it. Holding it matter of indifference whether he despatched this duty by night or by day, the Knife took it in hand at once, and set forth, on foot, with a letter for Colonel Digges, who lived about five miles off, at the same time that the other two couriers mounted their horses for their lonesome journeys through the forest.

CHAPTER VI

If we should wait till you, in solemn council
With due deliberation had selected
The smallest out of four and twenty evils,
'I faith we should wait long.
Dash and through with it—that's the better watchword,
Then after, come what may come.

Piccolomini.

On the following day, the council, consisting of some four or five gentlemen, were assembled at the Proprietary Mansion. About noon their number was rendered complete, by the arrival of Colonel George Talbot, who, mounted on a spirited, milk-white steed that smoked with the hot vigour of his motion, dashed through the gate and alighted at the door. A pair of pistols across his saddle-bow, and a poniard, partially disclosed under his vest, demonstrated the precautions of the possessor to defend himself against sudden assault, and no less denoted the quarrelsome aspect of the times. His frame was tall, athletic, and graceful; his eye hawk-like, and his features prominent and handsome, at the same time indicative of quick temper and rash resolve. There was in his dress a manifestation of the consciousness of a good figure—it was the costume of a gallant of the times; and his bearing was characteristic of a person accustomed to bold action and gay companionship.

Talbot was a near kinsman of the Baltimore family, and besides being a member of the Proprietary's council, he held the post of Surveyor General, and commanded, also, the provincial militia on the northern frontier, including the settlements on the Elk River, where he owned a large manor, upon which he usually resided. At the present time he was in the temporary occupation of a favourite seat of the Proprietary, at Mattapany on the Patuxent, whither the late summons had been despatched to call him to the council.

This gentleman was a zealous Catholic, and an ardent personal friend of his kinsman, the Proprietary, whose cause he advocated with that peremptory and, most usually, impolitic determination which his imperious nature prompted, and which served to draw upon him the peculiar hatred of Fendall and Coode, and their partisans. He was thus, although a sincere, it may be imagined, an indiscreet adviser in state affairs, little qualified to subdue or allay that jealous spirit of proscription which, from the epoch of the Protectorate down to this date, had been growing more intractable in the province.

Such was the individual who now with the firm stride and dauntless carriage of a belted and booted knight of chivalry, to which his picturesque costume heightened the resemblance, entered the apartment where his seniors were already convened.

"Well met!" he exclaimed, as he flung his hat and gloves upon a table and extended his hand to those who were nearest him. "How fares it, gentlemen? What devil of mutiny is abroad now? Has that pimpled fellow of fustian, that swiller of the leavings of a tap room, the worshipful king of the Burgesses, master Jack Coode, got drunk again and begun to bully in his cups? The falconer who hammered at my door last night, as if he would have beaten your Lordship's house about my ears, could tell me nothing of the cause of this sudden convocation, save that Driving Dick had come in hot haste from James Town with letters that had set the mansion here all agog, from his Lordship's closet down to the scullery."

"With proper abatement for the falconer's love of gossip," said the Proprietary, "he told you true. The letters are there on the table. When you have read them, you will see that with good reason I might make some commotion in my house."

Talbot ran his eye over the papers. "Well, and well—an old story!" he said, as he threw one letter aside and took up another. "Antichrist—the Red Lady of Babylon—the Jesuits—and the devil: we have had it so often that the lecture is somewhat stale. The truculent Papists are the authors of all evil! We had the Geneva band in fashion for a time; but that wore out with old Noll. And then comes another flight of kestrels, and we must have the thirty-nine articles served up for a daily dish. That spider, Master Yeo, has grown to be a crony of his grace the Archbishop of Canterbury, and is busy to knit his web around every poor catholic fly of the province."

"This must be managed without temper," said Darnall, the oldest member present, except the Chancellor. "Our adversaries will find their advantage in our resolves, if made in the heat of passion."

"You say true," replied Talbot. "I am a fool in my humour; but it doth move me to the last extremity of endurance to be ever goaded with this shallow and hypocritical pretence of sanctity. They prate of the wickedness of the province, forsooth! our evil deportment, and loose living, and notorious scandal! all will be cured, in the opinion of these solemn Pharisees, by turning that good man, Lord Charles and his friends out of his own province, and by setting up parson Yeo in a fat benefice under the wing of an established church."

"Read on," said Lord Baltimore, "and you shall see the sum of all, in the argument that it is not fit Papists should bear rule over the free-born subjects of the English crown; and, as a conclusion to that, a summary order to discharge every friend of our holy church from my employ."

Talbot read the letter to the end.

"So be it!" he ejaculated, as he threw the letter from him, and flung himself back into his chair. "You will obey this high behest? With all humbleness, we will thank these knaves for their many condescensions, and their good favours. Your uncle, the Chancellor here, our old frosted comrade, is the first that your Lordship will give bare-headed to the sky. As for myself, I have been voted an incarnate devil in a half dozen conclaves—and so Fendall shall be the surveyor. I hope your Lordship will remember that I have a military command—a sturdy stronghold in the fort of Christina—and some stout fellows with me on the border. It might be hard to persuade them to part company with me."

"Peace, I pray you, peace!" interrupted the Proprietary; "you are nettled, Talbot, and that is not the mood for counsel."

"These pious cut-throats here," said Talbot, "who talk of our degeneracy, slander us to the whole world: and, faith, I am not of the mind to bear it! I speak plainly what I have thought long since—and would rather do than speak. I would arrest the ring-leaders upon a smaller scruple of proof than I would set a vagrant in the stocks. You have Fendall now, my Lord—I would have his fellows before long: and the space between taking and trying should not add much to the length of their beards:—between trying and hanging, still less."

"As to that," said the Proprietary, "every day brings us fresh testimony of the sedition afoot, and we shall not be slow to do justice on the parties. We have good information of the extent of the plot against us, and but wait until an open act shall make their guilt unquestionable. Master Coode is now upon bail only because we were somewhat too hasty in his arrest. There are associates of Fendall's at work who little dream of our acquaintance with their designs."

"When does your provincial court hold its sessions?" inquired the Surveyor.

"In less than a month."

"It should make sure work and speedy," said Talbot. "Master Fendall should find himself at the end of his tether at the first sitting."

"Ay, and Coode too," said one of the council: "notwithstanding that the burgesses have stepped forward to protect him. The House guessed well of the temper against your Lordship in England, when they stood up so hardily, last month, in favour of Captain Coode, after your Lordship had commanded his expulsion. It was an unnatural contumacy."

"In truth, we have never had peace in the province," said another, "since Fendall was allowed to return from his banishment. That man hath set on hotter, but not subtler spirits than his own. He has a quiet craftiness which never sleeps nor loses sight of his purpose of disturbance."

"Alas!" said the Proprietary, "he has not lacked material to work with. The burgesses have been disaffected ever since my father's death. I know not in what point of kindness I have erred towards them. God knows I would cherish affection, not ill-will. My aim has ever been to do justice to all men."

"Justice is not their aim, my Lord," exclaimed Talbot. "Oh, this zeal for church is a pretty weapon! and honest Captain Coode, a dainty champion to handle it! I would cut the spurs from that fowl, if I did it with a cleaver!"

"He is but the fool in the hands of his betters," interposed Darnall. "This discontent has a broad base. There are many in the province who, if they will not take an open part against us, will be slow to rebuke an outbreak—many who will counsel in secret who dare not show their faces to the sun."

"These men have power to do us much harm," said Lord Baltimore, "and I would entreat you, gentlemen, consider, how, by concession to a moderate point, which may comport with our honour, we may allay these irritations. Leaving that question for your future advisement, I ask your attention to the letters. The King has commanded—for it is scarce less than a royal mandate."

"Your Lordship," said Talbot, sarcastically, "has fallen under his Majesty's disfavour. You have, doubtless, failed somewhat in your courtesies to Nell Gwynn, or the gay Duchess; or have been wanting in some observance of respect to old Tom Killigrew, the King's fool. His Majesty is not wont to look so narrowly into state affairs."

"Hold, Talbot!" interrupted the Proprietary. "I would not hear you speak slightingly of the King. He hath been friendly to me, and I will not forget it. Though this mandate come in his name, King Charles, I apprehend, knows but little of the matter. He has an easy conscience for an importunate suitor. Oh, it grieves me to the heart, after all my father's care for the province—and surely mine has been no less—it grieves me to see this wayward fortune coming over our hopes like a chill winter, when we looked for springtide, with its happy and cheerful promises. I am not to be envied for my prerogative. Here, in this new world, I have made my bed, where I had no wish but to lie in it quietly: it has become a bed of thorns, and cannot bring rest to me, until I am mingled with its dust. Well, since rebellion is the order of the times, I must e'en myself turn rebel now against this order."

"Wherein might it be obeyed, my Lord?" asked Darnall. "You have already given all the rights of conscience which the freemen could ask, and the demand now is that you surrender your own. What servant would your Lordship displace? Look around you: is Anthony Warden so incapable, or so hurtful to your service that you might find plea to dismiss him?"

"There is no better man in the province than Anthony Warden," replied the Proprietary, with warmth; "a just man; a good man in whatever duty you scan him; an upright, faithful servant to his post. My Lords of the Ministry would not and could not, if they knew him, ask me to remove that man. I will write letters back to remonstrate against this injustice."

"And say you will not displace a man, my Lord, come what may!" exclaimed Talbot. "This battle must be fought—and the sooner the better! Your Lordship will find your justification in the unanimous resolve of your council."

This sentiment was echoed by all present, and by some of the more discreet an admonition was added, advising the Proprietary to handle the subject mildly with the ministry, in a tone of kind expostulation, which, as it accorded with Lord Baltimore's own feeling, met his ready acquiescence.

After despatching some business of less concern, the members of the council dispersed.

CHAPTER VII

An old worshipful gentleman who had a great estate,
That kept a brave old house at a bountiful rate.
The Old and Young Courtier.

But who the countless charms can draw
That grac'd his mistress true?
Such charms the old world seldom saw,
Nor oft, I ween, the new.

Her raven hair plays round her neck
Like tendrils of the vine;
Her cheeks, red, dewy rose-buds deck,
Her eyes like diamonds shine.
Bryan and Pereene.

Anthony Warden had resided in Maryland for forty years before the period of this story. During the greater portion of this time he performed the duties of the Collector of the Proprietary's revenues in the port. By the persuasion of Cecilius Calvert he had become a settler in the New World, where he had received from his patron the grant of a large tract of land, which, in progress of time, under a careful course of husbandry, rendered him a man of easy fortune. One portion of this tract lay adjacent to the town, and stretched along the creek of St. Inigoe's, constituting an excellent farm of several hundred acres. Upon this land the Collector had dwelt from an early period of his settlement.

A certain sturdiness of character that matched the perils of that adventurous colonial life, and a vigorous intellect, gave Mr. Warden great authority over the inhabitants of the province, which was increased by the predominant honesty of purpose and plain, unpretending directness of his nature. A bountiful purse and jocund temper enabled and prompted him to indulge, almost without stint, that hospitality which furnishes the most natural and appropriate enjoyment of those who dwell remote from the busy marts of the world. His companionable habits had left their tokens upon his exterior. His frame was corpulent, his features strongly defined, his eye dark blue, with a mastiff kindness in its glance. The flush of generous living had slightly overmastered the wind-and-weather hue of his complexion, and given it the tints of a ripe pear. Seventy years had beaten upon his poll without other badge of conquest than that of a change of his brown locks to white;—their volume was scarcely diminished, and they still fell in curls upon his shoulders.

Two marriages had brought him a large family of children, of whom the eldest (the only offspring of his first nuptials) was Alice Warden, a maiden lady who now, well advanced in life, occupied the highest post of authority in the household, which had, for several years past, been transferred to her by the demise of the second wife. His sons had all abandoned the paternal roof in the various pursuits of fortune, leaving behind them, besides Mistress Alice, a sister, the youngest of the flock, who, at the epoch at which I am about to present her, was just verging towards womanhood.

The dwelling of the Collector stood upon the high bank formed by the union of St. Inigoe's creek and St. Mary's river. It was, according to the most approved fashion of that day, built of imported brick, with a double roof penetrated by narrow and triangular-capped windows. The rooms were large and embellished with carved wainscots and a profusion of chiseled woodwork, giving them an elaborate and expensive aspect. This main building overlooked, with a magisterial and protecting air, a group of single-storied offices and out-houses which were clustered around, one of which was appropriated by the Collector as his place of business, and may still be seen with its decayed book-shelves, a deserted ruin hard by the mansion which yet survives in tolerable repair. This spacious domicil, with its broad porch, cottage-like appendages and latticed sheds, was embosomed in the shade of elms and mulberries, whose brown foliage, fanned by the autumnal breeze, murmured in unison with the plashing tide that beat against the pebbles immediately below. A garden in the rear, with trellised and vine-clad gateways, and walks lined with box, which the traveller may yet behold in venerable luxuriance, furnished good store of culinary dainties; whilst a lawn, in front, occupying some two or three acres and bounded by the cliff which formed the headland on the river, lay open to the sun, and gave from the water an unobstructed view of the mansion. The taste displayed in these embellishments, the neatness of the grounds, the low, flower-spangled hedge of thorn that guarded the cliff, the clumps of rose trees and other ornamental shrubs, disposed to gratify the eye in the shifting seasons of their bloom, the various accessories of rustic seats, bowers and parterres—all united to present an agreeable and infallible index of that purity of mind which brought into assemblage such simple and attractive elements of beauty.

All around the immediate domain of the dwelling-house were orchards, woodlands and cultivated fields, with the usual barns and other structures necessary in the process of agriculture;—the whole region presenting a level plain, some fifty or sixty feet above the tide, of singular richness as a landscape, and no less agreeable to be looked upon for its associations with the idea of comfortable independence in the proprietor. This homestead had obtained the local designation of the Rose Croft,—a name, in some degree, descriptive of the predominant embellishment of the spot.

In his attire, Master Anthony Warden, the worshipful Collector (to give him his usual style of address in the province) exhibited some tendency towards the coxcombry of his day. It was marked by that scrupulous observance of the prerogative of rank and age which characterised the costume of the olden time,—smacking no little of the flavour of the official martinet. Authority, amongst our ancestors, was wont to borrow consequence from show. The broad line which separated gentle from simple was recognised, in those days, not less strongly in the habiliments of the person than in his nurture and manners. The divisions between the classes of society were not more authentically distinguished in any outward sign than in the embroidered velvet or cloth of the man of wealth, and the plain serge, worsted, or leather of the craftsman. The Collector of St. Mary's, on festive occasions, went forth arrayed much after the manner in which Leslie has represented Sir Roger de Coverly, in his admirable painting of that knight; and although he was too vain of his natural locks to adopt the periwig of that period, yet he had trained his luxuriant tresses into a studied imitation of this artificial adornment. His embroidered coat of drab velvet, with wadded skirts and huge open cuffs, his lace wristbands, his ample vest, and white lamb's-wool hose rolled above his knees, his buckled shoe and three-cornered hat—all adjusted with a particularity that would put our modern foppery to shame—gave to the worthy burgess of St. Mary's a substantial ascendancy and an unquestioned regard, that rendered him, next to the Proprietary, the most worshipful personage in the province.

This pedantry of costume and the circumspect carriage which it exacted, were pleasantly contrasted with the flowing vivacity of the wearer, engendering by their concourse an amusing compound, which I might call a fettered and pinioned alacrity of demeanour, the rigid stateliness of exterior seeming rather ineffectually to encase, as a half-bursting chrysalis, the wings of a gay nature.

Mr. Warden was reputed to be stubborn in opinion. The good people of the town, aware of his pertinacity in this particular, had no mind to make points with him, but, on the contrary, rather corroborated him in his dogmatism by an amiable assentation; so that, it is said, he grew daily more peremptory. This had become so much his prerogative, that the Lord Proprietary himself gave way to it with as good a grace as the rest of the inhabitants.

It may be imagined that so general a submission to this temper would have the tendency to render him a little passionate. They say it was a rich sight to see him in one of his flashes, which always took the bystanders by surprise, like thunder in the midst of sunshine; but these explosions were always short-lived, and rather left a more wholesome and genial clearness in the atmosphere of his affections.

The household at the Rose Croft, I have hinted, was regulated by Mistress Alice, who had, some time before our acquaintance with her, reached that period of life at which the female ambition for display is prone to subside into a love of domestic pursuits. It was now her chief worldly care and delight to promote the comfort of those who congregated around the family hearth. In the administration of this office, it may be told to her praise, that she manifested that unpretending good sense which is a much more rare and estimable quality than many others of better acceptation with the world. As was natural to her tranquil position and kindly temper, her feelings had taken a ply towards devotion, which father Pierre did not omit to encourage and confirm by all the persuasions enjoined by the discipline of the Romish church. The gentle solicitude with which the ministers of that ancient faith watch and assist the growing zeal of its votaries; the captivation of its venerable ceremonies, and the familiar and endearing tone in which it addresses itself to the regard of its children, sufficiently account for its sway over so large a portion of mankind, and especially for its hold upon the affections of the female breast.

Upon the thoughtful character of Alice Warden this influence shed a mellow and attractive light, and gave to the performance of her daily duties that orderly and uninterrupted cheerfulness which showed the content of her spirit. She found an engrossing labour of love in superintending the education of her sister. Blanche Warden had now arrived within a span of her eighteenth year. Alice had guarded her path from infancy with a mother's tenderness, ministering to her enjoyments and instilling into her mind all that her own attainments, circumscribed, it is true, within a narrow circle, enabled her to teach. The young favourite had grown up under this domestic nurture, aided by the valuable instructions of father Pierre, who had the guidance of her studies, a warm-hearted girl, accomplished much beyond the scant acquisitions ordinarily, at that day, within the reach of women, and distinguished for that confiding gentleness of heart and purity of thought and word which the caresses of friends, the perception of the domestic affections, and seclusion from the busy world are likely to engender in an ardent and artless nature.

Of the beauty of the Rose of St. Mary's (for so contemporaries were wont to designate her) tradition speaks with a poetical fervour. I have heard it said that Maryland, far-famed for lovely women, hath not since had a fairer daughter. The beauty which lives in expression was eminently hers; that beauty which is scarcely to be caught by the painter,—which, changeful as the surface of the welling fountain where all the fresh images of nature are for ever shifting and sparkling with the glories of the mirror, defies the limner's skill. In stature she was neither short nor tall, but distinguished by a form of admirable symmetry both for grace and activity. Her features, it is scarce necessary to say, were regular,—but not absolutely so, for, I know not why, perfect regularity is a hinderance to expression. Eyes of dark hazel, with long lashes that gave, by turns, a pensive and playful light to her face, serving, at will, to curtain from the world the thoughts which otherwise would have been read by friend and foe; hair of a rich brown, glossy and, in some lights, even like the raven's wing,—ample in volume and turning her brow and shoulders almost into marble by the contrast; a complexion of spotless, healthful white and red; a light, elastic step, responding to the gaiety of her heart; a voice melodious and clear, gentle in its tones and various in its modulation, according to the feeling it uttered;—these constituted no inconsiderable items in the inventory of her perfections. Her spirit was blithe, affectionate and quick in its sympathies; her ear credulous to believe what was good, and slow to take an evil report. The innocence of her thoughts kindled an habitual light upon her countenance, which was only dimmed when the rough handling by fortune of friend or kinsman was recounted to her, and brought forth the ready tear—for that was ever as ready as her smile.

I might tell more of Blanche Warden, but that my task compels me to hasten to the matter of my story.

CHAPTER VIII

The silk well could she twist and twine,
And make the fine march-pine,
And with the needle work:
And she could help the priest to say
His matins on a holiday
And sing a psalm in kirk.

Dowsabel.

With such attractions for old and young it will readily be believed that the Rose Croft was a favourite resort of the inhabitants of St. Mary's. The maidens gathered around Blanche as a May-day queen; the matrons possessed in Mistress Alice a discreet and kind friend, and the more sedate part of the population found an agreeable host in the worthy official himself.

The family of the Lord Proprietary sustained the most intimate relations with this household. It is true that Lady Baltimore, being feeble in health and stricken with grief at the loss of her son, which yet hung with scarcely abated poignancy upon her mind, was seldom seen beyond her own threshold; but his Lordship's sister, the Lady Maria—as she was entitled in the province—was a frequent and ever most welcome guest. Whether this good lady had the advantage of the Proprietary in years, would be an impertinent as well as an unprofitable inquiry, since no chronicler within my reach has thought fit to instruct the world on this point; and, if it were determined, the fact could neither heighten nor diminish the sober lustre of her virtues. Suffice it that she was a stirring, tidy little woman, who moved about with indefatigable zeal in the acquittal of the manifold duties which her large participation in the affairs of the town exacted of her—the Lady Bountiful of the province who visited the sick, fed the hungry, clothed the naked and chid the idle. She especially befriended such nursing-mothers as those whose scanty livelihood withheld from them the necessary comforts of their condition, and, in an equal degree, extended her bounty to such of the colonists as had been disabled in the military service of the province,—holding these two concerns of population and defence to be high state matters which her family connexion with the government most cogently recommended to her care. Though it is reported of her, that a constitutional tendency towards a too profuse distribution of nick-nacks and sweet-meats amongst her invalids, gave great concern and embarrassment to the physician of the town, and bred up between him and the lady a somewhat stubborn, but altogether good-natured warfare. She was wont to look in upon the provincial school-house, where, on stated occasions, she gave the young train-bands rewards for good conduct, and where she was also diligent to rebuke all vicious tendencies. In the early morning she tripped through the dew, with scrupulous regularity, to mass; often superintended the decorations of the chapel; gossiped with the neighbours after service, and, in short, kept her hands full of business.

Her interest in the comfort and welfare of the towns-people grew partly out of her temperament, and partly out of a feudal pride that regarded them as the liegemen of her brother the chief,—a relation which she considered as creating an obligation to extend to them her countenance upon all proper occasions: and, sooth to say, that countenance was not perhaps the most comely in the province, being somewhat sallow, but it was as full of benevolence as became so exemplary a spirit. She watched peculiarly what might be called the under-growth, and was very successful in worming herself into the schemes and plans of the young people. Her entertainments at the mansion were frequent, and no less acceptable to the gayer portion of the inhabitants than they were to her brother. On these occasions she held a little court, over which she presided with an amiable despotism, and fully maintained the state of the Lord Proprietary. By these means the Lady Maria had attained to an over-shadowing popularity in the town.

Blanche Warden had, from infancy, engaged her deepest solicitude; and as she took to herself no small share of the merit of that nurture by which her favourite had grown in accomplishment, she felt, in the maiden's praises which every where rang through the province, an almost maternal delight. Scarcely a day passed over without some manifestation of this concern. New patterns of embroidery, music brought by the last ship from *home*, some invitation of friendship or letter of counsel, furnished occasions of daily intercourse between the patroness and the maiden of the Rose Croft; and not unfrequently the venerable spinster herself,—attended by a familiar in the shape of a little Indian girl, Natta, the daughter of Pamesack, arrayed in the trinketry of her tribe—alighted from an ambling pony at the Collector's door, with a face full of the importance of business. Perchance, there might be an occasion of merry-making in contemplation, and then the lady Maria united in consultation with sister Alice concerning the details of the matter, and it was debated, with the deliberation due to so interesting a subject, whether Blanche should wear her black or her crimson velvet boddice, her sarsnet or her satin, and such other weighty matters as have not yet lost their claims to thoughtful consideration on similar emergencies.

In the frequent interchange of the offices of good neighbourhood between the families of the Proprietary and of the Collector, it could scarce fall out that the Secretary should not be a large participator. The shyness of the student and the habitual self-restraint taught him in the seminary of Antwerp, in some degree, screened from common observation the ardent character of Albert Verheyden. The deferential relation which he held to his patron threw into his demeanour a reserve expressive of humility rather than of diffidence; but under this there breathed a temperament deeply poetical and a longing for enterprise, that all the discipline of his school and the constraint of his position could scarce suppress. He was now at that time of life when the imagination is prone to dally with illusions; when youth, not yet yoked to the harness of the world's business, turns its spirit forth to seek adventure in the domain of fancy. He was thus far a dreamer, and dreamed of gorgeous scenes and bold exploits and rare fortune. He had the poet's instinct to perceive the beautiful, and his fancy hung it with richer garlands and charmed him into a worshipper. A mute worshipper he was, of the Rose of St. Mary's, from the first moment that he gazed upon her. That outward form of Blanche Warden, and the motion and impulses of that spirit, might not often haunt the Secretary's dream without leaving behind an image that should live for ever in his heart. To him the thought was enchantment, that in this remote wild, far away from the world's knowledge, a flower of such surpassing loveliness should drink the glorious light in solitude,—for so he, schooled in populous cities, deemed of this sequestered province,—and with this thought came breathings of poetry which wrought a transfiguration of the young votary and lifted him out of the sphere of this "working-day world." Day after day, week after week, and month after month, the Secretary watched the footsteps of the beautiful girl; but still it was silent, unpresuming adoration. It entered not into his mind to call it love: it was the very humbleness of devotion.

Meantime the maiden, unconscious of her own rare perfections and innocent of all thought of this secret homage, found Master Albert much the most accomplished and gentle youth she had ever seen. He had, without her observing how it became so, grown to be, in some relation or other, part and parcel of her most familiar meditations. His occasions of business with the Collector brought him so often to the Rose Croft that if they happened not every day, they were, at least, incidents of such common occurrence as to be noted by no ceremony—indeed rather to be counted on in the domestic routine. The Collector was apt to grow restless if, by any chance, they were suspended, as it was through the Secretary's mission he received the tidings of the time as well as the official commands of the Proprietary; whilst Albert's unobtrusive manners, his soft step and pretensionless familiarity with the household put no one out of the way to give him welcome. His early roaming in summer sometimes brought him, at sunrise, beneath the bank of the Rose Croft, where he looked, with the admiration of an artist, upon the calm waters of St. Inigoe's Creek, and upon the forest that flung its solemn shades over its farther shores. Not unfrequently, the fresh and blooming maiden had left her couch as early as himself, and tended her plants before the dew had left the leaves, and thus it chanced that she would find him in his vocation; and, like him, she took pleasure in gazing on that bright scene, when it was the delight of both to tell each other how beautiful it was. And when, in winter, the rain pattered from the eaves and the skies were dark, the Secretary, muffled in his cloak, would find his road to the Collector's mansion and help the maiden to while away the tedious time. Even "when lay the snow upon a level with the hedge," the two long miles of unbeaten track did not stop his visit, for the Secretary loved the adventure of such a journey; and Blanche often smiled to see how manfully he endured it, and how light he made of the snow-drift which the wind had sometimes heaped up into billows, behind which the feather of his bonnet might not be discovered while he sat upon his horse.

In this course of schooling Blanche and Albert grew into a near intimacy, and the maiden became dependent, for some share of her happiness, upon the Secretary without being aware. Master Albert had an exquisite touch of the lute and a rich voice to grace it, and Blanche found many occasions to tax his skill: he had a gallant carriage on horseback, and she needed the service of a cavalier: he was expert in the provincial sport of hawking, and had made such acquaintance with Blanche's merlin that scarce any one else could assist the maiden in casting off Ariel to a flight. In short, Blanche followed the bent of her own ingenuous and truthful nature, and did full justice to the Secretary's various capacity to please her, by putting his talents in requisition with an unchidden freedom, and without once pausing to explore the cause why Master Albert always came so opportunely to her thoughts. Doubtless, if she had had the wit to make this inquiry the charm of her liberty would have been broken, and a sentinel would, ever after, have checked the wandering of her free footstep.

The Collector, in regard to this intercourse, was sound asleep. His wise head was taken up with the concerns of the province, his estate, and the discussion of opinions that had little affinity to the topics likely to interest the meditations of a young maiden. He was not apt to see a love-affair, even if it lay, like a fallen tree, across his path, much less to hunt it out when it lurked like a bird amongst the flowers that grew in the shady coverts by the wayside. The astuteness of the lady Maria, however, was not so much at fault, and she soon discovered, what neither Blanche nor Albert had sufficiently studied to make them aware of their own category. But the Secretary was in favour with the lady Maria, and so, she kept her own counsel, as well as a good-natured watch upon the progress of events.

CHAPTER IX

Towards noon of the day on which the council held their session, a troop of maidens was seen issuing from the chapel. Their number might have been eight or ten. The orderly step with which they departed from the door was exchanged for a playful haste in grouping together when they got beyond the immediate precincts of the place of worship. Their buoyant carriage and lively gesticulations betokened the elasticity of health which was still more unequivocally shown in their ruddy complexions and well rounded forms.

Their path lay across the grassy plain towards the town, and passed immediately within the space embowered by an ancient, spreading poplar, scarce a hundred paces in front of the chapel. When the bevy reached this spot, they made a halt and gathered around one of their number, who seemed to be the object of a mirthful and rather tumultuary importunity. The individual thus beset was Blanche Warden. Together with a few elderly dames, who were at this moment standing at the door of the chapel in parley with father Pierre, this troop had constituted the whole congregation who had that morning attended the service of the festival of St. Bridget.

"Holy mother, how I am set upon!" exclaimed Blanche, as, half smiling and half earnest, she turned her back against the trunk of the tree. "Have I not said I could not? Why should my birth-day be so remembered that all the town must be talking about it?"

"You did promise," said one of the party, "or at least, Mistress Alice promised for you, full six months ago, that when you came to eighteen we should have a merry-making at the Rose Croft."

"It would not be seemly—I should be thought bold," replied the maiden, "to be turning my birth-day into a feast. Indeed, I must not and cannot, playmates."

"There is no must not nor cannot in our books, Blanche Warden," exclaimed another, "but simply we will. There is troth plighted for it, and that's enough for us. So we hold to that, good Blanche."

"Yes, good Blanche! gentle Blanche! sweetheart, we hold to that!" cried the whole party, in a clamorous onset.

"Truly, Grace Blackiston, you will have father Pierre checking us for noisy behaviour," said the maiden. "You see that he is now looking towards us. It is a pretty matter to make such a coil about! I marvel, has no one ever been eighteen before!"

"This day se'nnight," replied the arch girl to whom this reprimand was addressed, "will be the first day, Blanche Warden, the Rose of St. Mary's has ever seen eighteen; and it will be the last I trow: and what comes and goes but once in the wide world should be accounted a rare thing, and rarities should be noticed, sweetheart."

"If I was coming eighteen," said a damsel who scarce reached as high as Blanche's shoulder, "and had as pretty a house for a dance as the Rose Croft, there should be no lack of sport amongst the towns-people."

"It is easy to talk on a two year's venture, little Madge," replied Blanche; "for that is far enough off to allow space for boasting. But gently, dear playmates! do not clamour so loud. I would do your bidding with good heart if I thought it would not be called something froward in me to be noising my age abroad, as if it was my lady herself."

"We will advise with father Pierre and Lady Maria," responded Grace Blackiston; "they are coming this way."

At this moment the reverend priest, and the ladies with whom he had been in conversation, approached. The sister of the Proprietary was distinguished as well by her short stature and neat attire, as by her little Indian attendant, who followed bearing the lady's missal. The tall figure of father Pierre, arrayed in his black tunic and belt, towered above his female companions. He bore his square bonnet of black cloth in his hand, disclosing a small silk cap closely fitted to his crown, fringed around with the silver locks which, separating on his brow, gave the grace of age to a countenance full of benignity.

The presence of the churchman subdued the eager gaiety of the crowd, and two or three of the maidens ran up to him with an affectionate familiarity to make him acquainted with the subject of their contention.

"Father," said Grace Blackiston, "we have a complaint to lodge against Mistress Blanche for a promise-breaker. You must counsel her, father, to her duty."

"Ah, my child! pretty Blanche!" exclaimed the priest, with the alacrity of his native French temper, as he took the assailed damsel by the hand, "what have they to say against you? I will be your friend as well as your judge."

"The maidens, father," replied Blanche, "have taken leave of their wits, and have beset me like mad-caps to give them a dance at the Rose Croft on my birth-day. And I have stood on my refusal, father Pierre, as for a matter that would bring me into censure for pertness—as I am sure you will say it would—with worshipful people, that a damsel who should be modest in her behaviour, should so thrust herself forward to be observed."

"And we do not heed that, father Pierre," interrupted Grace Blackiston, who assumed to be the spokeswoman of the party, "holding it a scruple more nice than wise. Blanche has a trick of standing back more than a maiden needs. And, besides, we say that Mistress Alice is bound by pledge of word, and partly Blanche, too—for she stood by and said never a syllable against it—that we should have good cheer and dancing on that day at the Rose Croft. It is the feast of the blessed virgin, Terese, and we would fain persuade Blanche that the festival should be kept for the sake of her birth-day saint."

"My children," said the priest, who during this debate stood in the midst of the blooming troop, casting his glances from one to another with the pleased expression of an interested partaker of their mirth, and at the same time endeavouring to assume a countenance of mock gravity, "we will consider this matter with impartial justice. And, first, we will hear all that Mistress Blanche has to say. It is a profound subject. Do you admit the promise, my child?"

"I do not deny, father Pierre, that last Easter, when we met and danced at Grace Blackiston's, my sister Alice did make some promise, and I said nothing against it. But it was an idle speech of sister Alice, which I thought no more of till now; and now should not have remembered it if these wild mates of mine had not sung it in my ear with such clamour as must have made you think we had all gone mad."

"It is honestly confessed," said father Pierre; "and though I heard the outcry all the way to the church door, yet I did not deem the damsels absolutely mad, as you supposed. I am an old man, my child, and I have been taught by my experience, in what key seven, eight, or nine young girls will make known their desires when they are together: and, truly, it is their nature to speak all at the same time. They speak more than they listen—ha, ha! But we shall be mistaken if we conclude they are mad."

"Blanche, love," interposed the Lady Maria, "you have scarce given a good reason for gainsaying the wish of the damsels. Have a care, or you may find me a mutineer on this question."

"That's a rare lady—a kind lady!" shouted several. "Now, Blanche, you have no word of denial left."

"I am at mercy," said the maiden, "if my good mistress, the Lady Maria, is not content. Whatever my sister Alice and my father shall approve, and you, dear lady, shall say befits my state, that will I undertake right cheerfully. I would pleasure the whole town in the way of merry-making, if I may do so without seeming to set too much account upon so small a matter as my birth-day. I but feared it would not be well taken in one so young as I am."

"I will answer it to the town," said the Lady Maria. "It shall be done as upon my motion; and Mistress Alice shall take order in the matter as a thing wherein you had no part. Will that content you, Blanche?"

"I will be ruled in all things by my dear lady," replied the maiden. "You will speak to my father?"

"It shall be my special duty to look after it forthwith," responded the lady.

"Luckily," said father Pierre, laughing, "this great business is settled without the aid of the church. Well, I have lost some of my consequence in the winding up, and the Lady Maria is in the ascendant. I will have my revenge by being as merry as any of you at the feast. So, good day, mes enfants!"

With this sally, the priest left the company and retired to his dwelling hard by the chapel. The Lady Maria and her elderly companions moved towards the town, whilst the troop of damsels with increased volubility pursued their noisy triumph, and with rapid steps hastened to their several homes.

CHAPTER X

The Crow and Archer presented a busy scene on the evening of the day referred to in the last chapter. A report had been lately spread through the country that the brig Olive Branch,—an occasional trader between the province and the coasts of Holland and England—had arrived at St. Mary's. In consequence of this report there had been, during the last two days, a considerable accession to the usual guests of the inn, consisting of travellers both by land and water. Several small sloops and other craft had come into the harbour, and a half score inland proprietors had journeyed from their farms on horse-back, and taken up their quarters under the snug roof of Garret Weasel. The swarthy and gaunt watermen, arrayed in the close jackets and wide kilt-like breeches and in the parti-coloured, woollen caps peculiar to their vocation, were seen mingling in the tap-room with the more substantial cultivators of the soil. A few of the burghers of St. Mary's were found in the same groups, drawn thither by the love of company, the occasions, perchance, of business, or the mere attraction of an evening pot and pipe. The greater portion of this assemblage were loitering between the latticed bar of the common room, and the quay in front of the house, which had somewhat of the occupation and bustle of a little exchange. On a bench, in one corner of the tap-room, sat, in a ragged, patched coat resembling a pea-jacket, a saucy, vagrant-looking fiddler, conspicuous for a red face and a playful light blue eye; he wore a dingy, pliant white hat, fretted at the rim, set daintily on one side of his head, from beneath which his yellow locks depended over either cheek, completely covering his ears; and all the while scraped his begrimed and greasy instrument to a brisk tune, beating time upon the floor with a huge hob-nailed shoe. This personage had a vagabond popularity in the province under the name of Will of the Flats—a designation no less suited to his musical commodity than to the locality of his ostensible habitation, which was seated on the flats of Patuxent, not above fifteen miles from St. Mary's, where he was tenant of a few acres of barren marsh and a lodge or cabin not much larger than a good dog kennel.

Will's chief compeer and brother in taste and inclination, though of more affluent fortune, was Dick Pagan, or Driving Dick, according to his more familiar appellation, the courier who had lately brought the missives from James Town; a hard-favoured, weather-beaten, sturdy, little bow-legged fellow, in russet boots and long spurs, and wrapt in a coarse drab doublet secured by a leathern belt, with an immense brass buckle in front. Old Pamesack, likewise, formed a part of the group, and might have been observed seated on a settle at the door, quietly smoking his pipe, as unmoved by the current of idlers which ebbed and flowed past him, as the old barnacled pier of the quay by the daily flux and reflux of the river.

Such were the guests who now patronised the thriving establishment of Master Weasel. These good people were not only under the care, but also under the command of our hostess the dame Dorothy, who was a woman by no means apt to overlook her prerogative. The dame having been on a visit to a neighbour did not show herself in the tap-room until near the close of the day; in the mean time leaving her customers to the unchidden enjoyment of their entertainment which was administered by Matty Scamper,—a broad-chested, red-haired and indefatigable damsel, who in her capacity of adjutant to the hostess, had attained to great favour with the patrons of the tavern by her imperturbable good nature and ready answer to all calls of business. As for Master Weasel, never did pleasure-loving monarch more cheerfully surrender his kingdom to the rule of his minister than he to whatever power for the time was uppermost,—whether the dame herself, or her occasional vicegerent Matty of the Saucepan.

Matty's rule, however, was now terminated by the arrival of Mistress Weasel herself. It is fit I should give my reader some perception of the exterior of the hostess, as a woman of undoubted impression and consideration with the towns-people. Being now in her best attire which was evidently put on with a careful eye to effect, I may take occasion to say that one might suspect her of a consciousness of some deficiency of height, as well as of an undue breadth of figure, both which imperfections she had studied to conceal. She wore a high conical hat of green silk garnished with a band of pink ribbon which was set on by indentation or teethwise, and gathered in front into a spirited cluster of knots. Her jacket, with long tight sleeves, was also of green silk, adapted closely to her shape, now brought into its smallest compass by the aid of stays, and was trimmed in the same manner as the hat. A full scarlet petticoat reached within a span of her ankles and disclosed a buxom, well-formed leg in brown stocking with flashy clocks of thickly embossed crimson, and a foot, of which the owner had reason to be proud, neatly pinched into a green shoe with a tottering high heel. Her black hair hung in plaits down her back; and her countenance,—distinguished by a dark waggish eye, a clear complexion, and a turned-up nose, to which might be added a neck both fat and fair, half concealed by a loose kerchief,—radiated with an expression partly wicked and partly charitable, but in every lineament denoting determination and constancy of purpose.

This air of careless boldness was not a little heightened by the absence of all defence to her brow from the narrow rim of the hat and the height at which it was elevated above her features.

The din of the tap-room was hushed into momentary silence as soon as this notable figure appeared on the threshold.

"Heaven help these thirsty, roystering men!" she exclaimed, as she paused an instant at the door and surveyed the group within—"On my conscience, they are still at it as greedily as if they had just come out of a dry lent! From sunrise till noon, and from noon till night it is all the same—drink, drink, drink. Have ye news of Master Cocklescraft?—I would that the Olive Branch were come and gone, that I might sit under a quiet roof again!—there is nothing but riot and reeling from the time the skipper is expected in the port until he leaves it."

"True enough, jolly queen!" said Ralph Haywood, a young inland planter, taking the hand of the merry landlady as she struggled by him on her way to the bar—"what the devil, in good earnest, has become of Cocklescraft? This is the second day we have waited for him. I half suspect you, mistress, of a trick to gather good fellows about you, by setting up a false report of the Olive Branch."

"Thou art a lying varlet, Ralph," quickly responded the dame: "you yourself came jogging hither with the story that Cocklescraft was seen two days ago, beating off the Rappahannock.—I play a trick on you, truly! You must think I have need of custom, to bring in a troop of swilling bumpkins from the country who would eat and drink out the character of any reputable house in the hundred, without so much as one doit of profit. You have my free leave to tramp it back again to Providence, Ralph Haywood, whenever you have a mind."

"Nay, now you quarrel with an old friend, Mistress Dorothy."

"Take thy hand off my shoulder, Ralph, thou coaxing villain!—Ha, ha, I warrant you get naught but vinegar from me, for your treacle.—But come—thou art a good child, and shalt have of the best in this house:—I would only warn you to call for it mannerly, Master Ralph."

"Our dame is a woman of mettle," said another of the company, as the landlady escaped from the planter and took her station behind the bar.

"What has become of that man Weasel?" she inquired somewhat petulantly. "The man I am sure has been abroad ever since I left the house! He is of no more value than a cracked pot;—he would see me work myself as thin as a broom handle before he would think of turning himself round."

"Garret is now upon the quay," replied one of the customers;—"I saw him but a moment since with Arnold the Ranger."

"With some idle stroller,—you may be sure of that!" interrupted the hostess:—"never at his place, if the whole house should go dry as Cuthbert's spring at midsummer. Call him to me, if you please, Master Shortgrass.—Michael Curtis, that wench Matty Scamper has something to do besides listen to your claverings! Matty, begone to the kitchen; these country cattle will want their suppers presently.—Oh, Willy, Willy o' the Flats!—for the sake of one's ears, in mercy, stop that everlasting twangling of your old crowd!—It would disgrace the patience of any Christian woman in the world to abide in the midst of all this uproar!—Nay then, come forward, old crony—I would not offend thee," she said in a milder tone to the fiddler. "Here is a cup of ale for thee, and Matty will give you your supper to-night. I have danced too often to thy music to deny thee a comfort;—so, drink as you will! but pray you rest your elbow for a while."

"And there is a shilling down on the nail," said Driving Dick, as he and the crowder came together to the bar at the summons of the landlady: "when that is drunk out, dame, give me a space of warning, that I may resolve whether we shall go another shot."

"Master Shortgrass told me you had need of me," said Garret Weasel, as he now entered the door;—"what wouldst with me, wife Dorothy?"

"Get you gone!" replied the wife—"thou art ever in the way. I warrant your head is always thrust in place when it is not wanted! If you had been at your duty an hour ago, your service might have been useful."

"I can but return to the quay," said Garret, at the same time beginning to retrace his steps.

"Bide thee!" exclaimed the dame in a shrill voice—"I have occasion for you. Go to the cellar and bring up another stoop of hollands; these salt water fish have no relish for ale—they must deal in the strong:—nothing but hollands or brandy for them."

The obedient husband took the key of the cellar and went on the duty assigned him.

At this moment a door communicating with an adjoining apartment was thrown ajar and the head of Captain Dauntrees protruded into the tap-room.

"Mistress Dorothy," he said—"at your leisure, pray step this way."

The dame tarried no longer than was necessary to complete a measure she was filling for a customer, and then went into the room to which she had been summoned. This was a little parlour, where the Captain of musqueteers had been regaling himself for the last hour over a jorum of ale, in solitary rumination. An open window gave to his view the full expanse of the river, now glowing with the rich reflexions of sunset; and a balmy October breeze played through the apartment and refreshed without chilling the frame of the comfortable Captain. He was seated near the window in a large easy chair when the hostess entered.

"Welcome dame," he said, without rising from his seat, at the same time offering his hand, which was readily accepted by the landlady.—"By St. Gregory and St. Michael both, a more buxom and tidy piece of flesh and blood hath never sailed between the two headlands of Potomac, than thou art! You are for a junketing, Mistress Dorothy; you are tricked out like a queen this evening! I have never seen thee in thy new suit before. Thou art as gay as a marygold: and I wear thy colours, thou laughing mother of mischief! Green is the livery of thy true knight. Has your goodman, honest Garret, come home yet, dame?"

"What would you with my husband, Master Baldpate? There is no good in the wind when you throw yourself into the big chair of this parlour."

"In truth, dame, I only came to make a short night of it with you and your worthy spouse. Do not show your white teeth at me, hussy,—you are too old to bite. Tell Matty to spread supper for me in this parlour. Arnold and Pamesack will partake with me; and if the veritable and most authentic head of this house—I mean yourself, mistress—have no need of Garret, I would entreat to have him in company. By the hand of thy soldier, Mistress Dorothy! I am glad to see you thrive so in your calling. You will spare me Garret, dame? Come, I know you have not learnt how to refuse me a boon."

"You are a saucy Jack, Master Captain," replied the dame. "I know you of old: you would have a rouse with that thriftless babe my husband. You sent him reeling home only last night. How can you look me in the face, knowing him, as you do, for a most shallow vessel, Captain Dauntrees?"

"Fie on thee, dame! You disgrace your own flesh and blood by such speech. Did you not choose him for his qualities?—ay, and with all circumspection, as a woman of experience. You had two husbands before Garret, and when you took him for a third, it was not in ignorance of the sex. Look thee in the face! I dare,—yea, and at thy whole configuration. Faith, you wear most bravely, Mistress Weasel! Stand apart, and let me survey: turn thy shoulders round," he added, as by a sleight he twirled the dame upon her heel so as to bring her back to his view—"thou art a woman of ten thousand, and I envy Garret such store of womanly wealth."

"If Garret were the man I took him for, Master Captain," said the dame with a saucy smile, "you would have borne a broken head long since. But he has his virtues, such as they are,—though they may lie in an egg-shell: and Garret has his frailties too, like other men: alack, there is no denying it!"

"Frailties, forsooth! Which of us has not, dame? Garret is an honest man;—somewhat old—a shade or so: yet it is but a shade. For my sake, pretty hostess, you will allow him to sup with us? Speak it kindly, sweetheart—good, old Garret's jolly, young wife!"

"Thou wheedling devil!" said the landlady; "Garret is no older than thou art. But, truly, I may say he is of little account in the tap-room; so, he shall come to you, Captain. But, look you, he is weak, and must not be over-charged."

"He shall not, mistress—you have a soldier's word for that. I could have sworn you would not deny me. Hark you, dame,—bring thine ear to my lips;—a word in secret."

The hostess bent her head down, as the Captain desired, when he said in a half whisper, "Send me a flask of the best,—you understand? And there's for thy pains!" he added, as he saluted her cheek with a kiss.

"And there's for thy impudence, saucy Captain!" retorted the spirited landlady as she bestowed the palm of her hand on the side of his head and fled out of the apartment.

Dauntrees sprang from his chair and chased the retreating dame into the midst of the crowd of the tap-room, by whose aid she was enabled to make her escape. Here he encountered Garret Weasel, with whom he went forth in quest of Arnold and the Indian, who were to be his guests at supper.

In the course of the next half hour the Captain and his three comrades were assembled in the little parlour around the table, discussing their evening meal. When this was over, Matty was ordered to clear the board and to place a bottle of wine and glasses before the party, and then to leave the room.

"You must know, Garret," said Dauntrees when the serving-maid had retired, "that we go to-night to visit the Wizard's Chapel by his Lordship's order; and as I would have stout fellows with me, I have come down here on purpose to take you along."

"Heaven bless us, Master Jasper Dauntrees!" exclaimed Garret, somewhat confounded with this sudden appeal to his valour, which was not of that prompt complexion to stand so instant a demand, and yet which the publican was never willing to have doubted—"truly there be three of you, and it might mar the matter to have too many on so secret an outgoing"——

"Tush, man,—that has been considered. His Lordship especially looks to your going: you cannot choose but go."

"But my wife, Captain Dauntrees"——

"Leave that to me," said the Captain; "I will manage it as handsomely as the taking of Troy. Worthy Garret, say naught against it—you must go, and take with you a few bottles of Canary and a good luncheon of provender in the basket. You shall be our commissary. I came on set purpose to procure the assistance of your experience, and store of comfortable sustenance. Get the bottles, Garret,—his Lordship pays the scot to-night."

"I should have my nag," said Garret, "and the dame keeps the key of the stable, and will in no wise consent to let me have it. She would suspect us for a rouse if I but asked the key."

"I will engage for that, good Weasel," said Dauntrees: "I will cozen the dame with some special invention which shall put her to giving the key of her own motion: she shall be coaxed with a device that shall make all sure—only say you will obey his Lordship's earnest desire."

"It is a notable piece of service," said the innkeeper, meditating over the subject, and tickled with the importance which was ascribed to his cooperation—"and will win thanks from the whole province. His Lordship did wisely to give it in charge to valiant men."

"In faith did he," replied the Captain; "and it will be the finishing stroke of thy fortunes. You will be a man of mark for ever after."

"I am a man to be looked to in a strait, Captain," said Weasel, growing valorous with the thought. "I saw by his Lordship's eye yesternight that he was much moved by what I told him. I have had a wrestle with devils before now."

Arnold smiled and cast his eye towards the Indian, who, immediately after supper, had quitted the table and taken a seat in the window.

"There be hot devils and cold devils," said he, "and he that wrestles with them must have a hand that will hold fire as well as ice: that is true, Pamesack?"

"Pamesack has no dealing with the white man's devil," replied the Indian; "he has enough to do with his own."

"Drink some wine, old blade," said Dauntrees as he presented a cup to Pamesack; "the Knife must be sharp to-night—this will whet his edge. We shall have need of your woodcraft."

The Indian merely sipped the wine, as he replied, "Pamesack knows the broad path and the narrow both. He can lead you to the Black House day or night."

"Brandy is more natural to his throat than this thin drink," said Weasel, who forthwith left the room and returned with a measure of the stronger liquor. When this was presented Pamesack swallowed it at a draught, and with something approaching a laugh, he said, "It is the white man's devil—but the Indian does not fear him."

"Now, Garret," said Dauntrees, "we have no time to lose. Make ready your basket and bottles, and lay them at the foot of the cedar below the bank, near the Town House steps; then hasten back to the parlour. I will put the dame to sending you on an errand which may be done only on horseback;—you will mount with the basket and make speedy way to the Fort. Tell Nicholas Verbrack, the lieutenant, that I shall be there in reasonable time. We must set forth by ten; it may take us three hours to reach St. Jerome's."

"My heart is big enough," said Weasel, once more beginning to waver, "for any venture; but, in truth, I fear the dame. It will be a livelong night carouse, and she is mortal against that. What will she say in the morning?"

"What can she say, when all is come and gone, but, perchance, that thou wert rash and hot-headed? That will do you no harm: but an hour ago she swore to me that you were getting old—and sighed too, as if she believed her words."

"Old, did she say? Ho, mistress, I will show you my infirmities! A fig for her scruples! the hey-day blood yerks yet, Master Captain. I will go with thee, comrades: I will follow you to any goblin's chapel twixt St. Mary's and Christina."

"Well said, brave vintner!" exclaimed the Captain; "now stir thee! And when you come back to the parlour, Master Weasel, you shall find the dame here. Watch my eye and take my hint, so that you play into my hand when need shall be. I will get the nag out of the stable if he were covered with bells. Away for the provender!"

The publican went about his preparations, and had no sooner left the room than the Captain called the landlady, who at his invitation showed herself at the door.

"Come in, sweetheart. Good Mistress Daffodil," he said, "I called you that you may lend us your help to laugh: since your rufflers are dispersed, your smokers obnubilated in their own clouds, your tipplers strewed upon the benches, and nothing more left for you to do in the tap-room, we would have your worshipful and witty company here in the parlour. So, come in, my princess of pleasant thoughts, and make us merry with thy fancies."

"There is nothing but clinking of cans and swaggering speeches where you are, Captain Dauntrees," said the hostess. "An honest woman had best be little seen in your company. It is a wonder you ever got out of the Low Countries, where, what with drinking with boors and quarrelling with belted bullies, your three years' service was enough to put an end to a thousand fellows of your humour."

"There's destiny in it, dame. I was born to be the delight of your eyes. It was found in my horoscope, when my nativity was cast, that a certain jolly mistress of a most-especially-to-be-commended inn, situate upon a delectable point of land in the New World, was to be greatly indebted to me, first, for the good fame of her wines amongst worshipful people; and, secondly, for the sufficient and decent praise of her beauty. So was it read to my mother by the wise astrologer. And then, dame, you slander the virtue of the Low Countries. Look at Arnold there: is there a more temperate, orderly, well-behaved liegeman in the world than the ranger? And did he not bring his sobriety with him from the very bosom of the land you rail against?"

"If Arnold de la Grange is not all that you say of him," replied the hostess, "it is because he has lost some share of his good quality by consorting with you, Captain. Besides, Arnold has never been hackneyed in the wars."

"A Dutch head," said Arnold, laughing, "is not easily made to spin. In the Old World men can drink more than in the New: a Friesland fog is an excellent shaving horn, mistress!"

"Heaven help the men of the Old World, if they drink more than they do in our province!" exclaimed Mistress Weasel. "Look in the tap-room, and you may see the end of a day's work in at least ten great loons. One half are sound asleep, and the other of so dim sight that neither can see his neighbour."

"The better reason then, Mistress Dorothy," replied Dauntrees, "why you, a reputable woman, should leave such topers, and keep company with sober, waking, discreet friends. That cap becomes thee, mistress. I never saw you in so dainty a head-gear. I honour it as a covering altogether worthy of thy comeliness. Faith, it has been a rich piece of merchandise to me! Upon an outlay of fourteen shillings which I paid for it, as a Michaelmas present to my excellent hostess, I have got in return, by way of profit, full thirteen bottles of Garret's choicest Canary, on my wager. Garret was obstinate, and would face me out with it that you wore it to church last Sunday, when I knew that you went only in your hood that day:—he has never an eye to look on thee, dame, as he ought,—so he must needs put it to a wager. Well, as this is the first day thou hast ever gone abroad in it, here I drink to thee and thy cap, upon my knees—Success to its travels, and joy to the merry eye that sparkles below it! Come, Arnold, drink to that, and get Pamesack another glass of aqua vitæ:—top off to the hostess, comrades!"

The toast was drunk, and at this moment Garret Weasel returned to the room. A sign from him informed the Captain that the preparation he had been despatched to make was accomplished.

"How looks the night, Garret?" inquired Dauntrees; "when have we the moon?"

"It is a clear starlight and calm," replied the publican; "the moon will not show herself till near morning."

"Have you heard the news, mistress?" inquired the Captain, with an expression of some eagerness; "there is pleasant matter current, concerning the mercer's wife at the Blue Triangle. But you must have heard it before this?"

"No, truly, not I," replied the hostess.

"Indeed!" said Dauntrees, "then there's a month's amusement for you. You owe the sly jade a grudge, mistress."

"In faith I do," said the dame, smiling, "and would gladly pay it."

"You may pay it off with usury now," added the Captain, "with no more trouble than telling the story. It is a rare jest, and will not die quickly."

"I pray you tell it to me, good Captain—give me all of it," exclaimed the dame, eagerly.

"Peregrine Cadger, the mercer, you know," said the Captain—"but it is a long story, and will take time to rehearse it. Garret, how comes it that you did not tell this matter to your wife, as I charged you to do?" he inquired, with a wink at the publican.

"I resolved to tell it to her," said Weasel, "but, I know not how, it ran out of my mind—the day being a busy one——"

"A busy day to thee!" exclaimed the spouse. "Thou, who hast no more to do than a stray in the pound, what are you fit for, if it be not to do as you are commanded? But go on, Captain; the story would only be marred by Garret's telling—go on yourself—I am impatient to hear it."

"I pray you, what o'clock is it, mistress?" asked the Captain.

"It is only near nine. It matters not for the hour—go on."

"Nine!" exclaimed Dauntrees; "truly, dame, I must leave the story for Master Garret. Nine, said you? By my sword, I have overstaid my time! I have business with the Lord Proprietary before he goes to his bed. There are papers at the Fort which should have been delivered to his Lordship before this."

"Nay, Captain," said the hostess, "if it be but the delivery of a pacquet, it may be done by some other hand. There is Driving Dick in the tap-room: he shall do your bidding in the matter. Do not let so light a business as that take you away."

"To-morrow, dame, and I will tell you the tale."

"To-night, Captain—to-night."

"Truly, I must go; the papers should be delivered by a trusty hand—I may not leave it to an ordinary messenger. Now if Garret—but I will ask no such service from the good man at this time of night; it is a long way. No, no, I must do my own errand."

"There is no reason upon earth," said the landlady, "why Garret should not do it: it is but a step to the Fort and back."

"I can take my nag and ride there in twenty minutes," said Garret. "I warrant you his Lordship will think the message wisely entrusted to me."

"Then get you gone, without parley," exclaimed the dame.

"The key of the stable, wife," said Garret.

"If you will go, Master Garret," said Dauntrees—"and it is very obliging of you—do it quickly. Tell Nicholas Verbrack to look in my scritoire; he will find the pacquet addressed to his Lordship. Take it, and see it safely put into his Lordship's hands. Say to Nicholas, moreover, that I will be at the Fort before ten to-night. You comprehend?"

"I comprehend," replied Garret, as his wife gave him the key of the stable, and he departed from the room.

"Now, Captain."

"Well, mistress: you must know that Peregrine Cadger, the mercer, who in the main is a discreet man——"

"Yes."

"A discreet man—I mean, bating some follies which you wot of; for this trading and trafficking naturally begets foresight. A man has so much to do with the world in that vocation, and the world, Mistress Dorothy, is inclined by temper to be somewhat knavish, so that they who have much to do with it learn cautions which other folks do not. Now, in our calling of soldiership, caution is a sneaking virtue which we soon send to the devil; and thereby you may see how it is that we are more honest than other people. Caution and honesty do not much consort together."

"But of the mercer's wife, Captain."

"Ay, the mercer's wife—I shall come to her presently. Well, Peregrine, as you have often seen, is a shade or so jealous of that fussock, his wife, who looks, when she is tricked out in her new russet grogram cloak, more like a brown haycock in motion than a living woman."

"Yes," interrupted the dame, laughing, "and with a sunburnt top. Her red hair on her shoulders is no better, I trow."

"Her husband, who at best is but a cotquean—one of those fellows who has a dastardly fear of his wife, which, you know, Mistress Dorothy, truly makes both man and wife to be laughed at. A husband should have his own way, and follow his humour, no matter whether the dame rails or not. You agree with me in this, Mistress Weasel?"

"In part, Captain. I am not for stinting a husband in his lawful walks; but the wife should have an eye to his ways: she may counsel him."

"Oh, in reason, I grant; but she should not chide him, I mean, nor look too narrowly into his hours, that's all. Now Peregrine's dame hath a free foot, and the mercer himself somewhat of a sulky brow. Well, Halfpenny, the chapman, who is a mad wag for mischief, and who is withal a sure customer of the mercer's in small wares, comes yesternight to Peregrine Cadger's house, bringing with him worshipful Master Lawrence Hay, the Viewer."

At this moment the sound of horse's feet from the court-yard showed that Garret Weasel had set forth on his ride.

"Arnold, I am keeping you waiting," said Dauntrees. "Fill up another cup for yourself and Pamesack, and go your ways. Stay not for me, friends; or if it pleases you, wait for me in the tap-room. I will be ready in a brief space."

The ranger and the Indian, after swallowing another glass, withdrew.

"The Viewer," continued Dauntrees, "is a handsome man,—and a merry man on occasion, too. I had heard it whispered before—but not liking to raise a scandal upon a neighbour, I kept my thoughts to myself—that the mercer's wife had rather a warm side for the Viewer. But be that as it may: there was the most laughable prank played on the mercer by Halfpenny and the Viewer together, last night, that ever was heard of. It was thus: they had a game at Hoodman-blind, and when it fell to Lawrence to be the seeker, somehow the fat termagant was caught in his arms, and so the hood next came to her. Well, she was blindfolded; and there was an agreement all round that no one should speak a word."

"Ay, I understand—I see it," said the hostess, eagerly drawing her chair nearer to the Captain.

"No, you would never guess," replied Dauntrees, "if you cudgelled your brains from now till Christmas. But I can show you, Mistress Dorothy, better by the acting of the scene. Here, get down on your knees, and let me put your kerchief over your eyes."

"What can that signify?" inquired the dame.

"Do it, mistress—you will laugh at the explosion. Give me the handkerchief. Down, dame, upon your marrow bones:—it is an excellent jest and worth the learning."

The landlady dropped upon her knees, and the Captain secured the bandage round her eyes.

"How many fingers, dame?" he asked, holding his hand before her face.

"Never a finger can I see, Captain."

"It is well. Now stand up—forth and away! That was the word given by the Viewer. Turn, Mistress Dorothy, and grope through the room. Oh, you shall laugh at this roundly. Grope, grope, dame."

The obedient and marvelling landlady began to grope through the apartment, and Dauntrees, quietly opening the door, stole off to the tap-room, where being joined by his comrades, they hied with all speed towards the Fort, leaving the credulous dame floundering after a jest, at least until they got beyond the hail of her voice.

CHAPTER XI

Pale lights on Cadez' rocks were seen,.
And midnight voices heard to moan,.
'Twas even said the blasted oak,.
Convulsive heaved a hollow groan..
And to this day the peasant still,.
With cautious fear avoids the ground,.
In each wild branch a spectre sees.
And trembles at each rising ground.

The Spirit's Blasted Tree.

Dauntrees, after his unmannerly escape from the credulous landlady, hastened with his two companions, at a swinging gate, along the beach to the fort, where they found Garret Weasel waiting for them in a state of eager expectation.

"Is the dame likely to be angry, Captain?" were the publican's first words.—"Does she suspect us for a frisk to-night? Adsheartlikens, it is a perilous adventure for the morrow! You shall bear the burden of that reckoning, Master Captain."

"I left Mistress Dorothy groping for a secret at Hoodman-blind," replied the Captain, laughing. "She has found it before now, and by my computation is in the prettiest hurricane that ever brought a frown upon a woman's brow. She would bless the four quarters of thee, Garret, if thou shouldst return home to-night, with a blessing that would leave a scorch-mark on thee for the rest of thy days. I shouldn't wonder presently to hear her feet pattering on the gravel of the beach in full pursuit of us—dark as it is: I have left her in a mood to tempt any unheard of danger for revenge. So, let us be away upon our errand. You have the eatables safe and the wine sound, worthy Weasel?—Nicholas," he said, speaking to the Lieutenant—"are our horses saddled?"

"They are at the post on the other side of the parade," replied the Lieutenant.

"Alack!" exclaimed Weasel—"Alack for these pranks! Here will be a week's repentance. But a fig for conclusions!—in for a penny, in for a pound, masters. I have the basket well stored and in good keeping. It will be discreet to mount quickly—I will not answer against the dame's rapping at the gate to-night: she is a woman of spirit and valiant in her anger."

"Then let us be up and away," said the Captain, who was busily bestowing a pair of pistols in his belt and suspending his sword across his body.

"A cutlass and pistols for me," said the publican, as he selected his weapons from several at hand.

Arnold and Pamesack were each provided with a carbine, when Dauntrees, throwing his cloak across his shoulders, led the way to the horses, where the party having mounted, sallied through the gate of the fort at a gallop.

Their road lay around the head of St. Inigoe's creek, and soon became entangled in dark, woody ravines and steep acclivities which presented, at this hour, no small interruption to their progress. Pamesack, on a slouching pony, his legs dangling within a foot of the ground, led the way with an almost instinctive knowledge of his intricate path, which might have defied a darker night. The stars shining through a crisp and cloudless atmosphere, enabled the party to discern the profile of the tree tops, and disclosed to them, at intervals, the track of this solitary road with sufficient distinctness to prevent their entirely losing it.

They had journeyed for more than two hours in the depths of the forest before they approached the inlet of St. Jerome's. Dauntrees had beguiled the time by tales of former adventures, and now and then by sallies of humour provoked by the dubious valour of the innkeeper,—for Weasel, although addicted to the vanity of exhibiting himself in the light of a swashing, cut-and-thrust comrade in an emprise of peril, was nevertheless unable, this night, to suppress the involuntary confession of a lurking faint-heartedness at the result of the present venture. This inward misgiving showed itself in his increased garrulity and in the exaggerated tone of his vauntings of what he had done in sundry emergencies of hazard, as well as of what he had made up his mind to do on the present occasion if they should be so fortunate as to encounter any peculiarly severe stress of fortune. Upon such topics the party grew jovial and Dauntrees laughed at the top of his voice.

"The vintner's old roystering courses would make us lose our road in downright blindness from laughing," he said, as checking himself in one of these out-breaks, he reined up his horse. "Where are we, Pamesack? I surely hear the stroke of the tide upon the beach;—are we so near St. Jerome's, or have we missed the track and struck the bay shore short of our aim?"

"The she-fox does not run to her den where she has left her young, by a track more sure than mine to-night," replied the guide:—"it is the wave striking upon the sand at the head of the inlet: you may see the stars on the water through yonder wood."

"Pamesack says true," added Arnold. "He has found his way better than a hound."

A piece of cleared land, or old field, a few acres in width, lay between the travellers and the water which began now to glimmer on their sight through a fringe of wood that grew upon the margin of the creek or inlet, and the fresh breeze showed that the broad expanse of the Chesapeake was at no great distance.

"The Wizard's Chapel," said Dauntrees, "by my reckoning then, should be within a mile of this spot. It were a good point of soldiership to push forward a vanguard. That duty, Garret, will best comport with your mad-cap humour—there may be pith in it: so, onward, man, until you are challenged by some out-post of the Foul One—we will tarry here for your report. In the mean time, leave us your hamper of provender. Come, man of cold iron, be alert—thy stomach is growing restive for a deed of valour."

"You are a man trained to pike and musquetoon," replied the publican; "and have the skill to set a company, as men commonly fight with men. But I humbly opine, Captain, that our venture to-night stands in no need of vanguard, patrol or picquet. We have unearthly things to wrestle with, and do not strive according to the usages of the wars. I would not be slow to do your bidding, but that I know good may not come of it: in my poor judgment we should creep towards the Chapel together, not parting company. I will stand by thee, Captain, with a sharp eye and ready hand."

"Thy teeth will betray us, Master Vintner, even at a score rods from the enemy," said Dauntrees: "they chatter so rudely that thy nether jaw is in danger. If thou art cold, man, button up thy coat."

"Of a verity it is a cold night, and my coat is none of the thickest," replied Weasel with an increasing shudder.

"I understand you, Garret," responded the Captain with a laugh; "we must drink. So, friends, to the green grass, and fasten your horses to the trees whilst we warm up the liver of our forlorn vintner with a cup. We can all take that physic."

This command was obeyed by the immediate dismounting of the party and their attack upon one of the flasks in the basket.

"It has a rare smack for a frosty night," said Dauntrees as he quaffed a third and fourth cup. "When I was in Tours I visited the abbey of Marmoustier, and there drank a veritable potation from the huge tun which the blessed St. Martin himself filled, by squeezing a single cluster of grapes. It has the repute of being the kindliest wine in all Christendom for the invigorating of those who are called to do battle with the devil. The monks of the abbey have ever found it a most deadly weapon against Satan. And truly, Master Weasel, if I did not know that this wine was of the breed of the islands, I should take it to be a dripping from the holy tun I spoke of:—it hath the like virtue of defiance of Beelzebub. So, drink—drink again, worthy purveyor and valiant adjutant!"

"What is that?" exclaimed Weasel, taking the cup from his lips before he had finished the contents. "There is something far off like the howl of a dog and yet more devilish I should say—did ye not hear it, masters? I pray heaven there be no evil warning in this:—I am cold—still cold, Captain Dauntrees."

"Tush, it is the ringing of your own ears, Garret, or it may be, like enough, some devil's cur that scents our footsteps. Make yourself a fire, and whilst you grow warm by that grosser element we will take a range, for a brief space, round the Chapel. You shall guard the forage till we return."

"That is well thought of," replied the innkeeper quickly. "Light and heat will both be useful in our onslaught:—while you three advance towards the shore I will keep a look out here; for there is no knowing what devices the enemy may have a-foot to take us by surprise."

Some little time was spent in kindling a fire, which had no sooner begun to blaze than Dauntrees, with the Ranger and the Indian, set forth on their reconnoissance of the Chapel, leaving Weasel assured that he was rendering important service in guarding the provender and comforting himself by the blazing fagots.

They walked briskly across the open ground towards the water, and as they now approached the spot which common rumour had invested with so many terrors, even these bold adventurers themselves were not without some misgivings. The universal belief in supernatural agencies in the concerns of mankind, which distinguished the era of this narrative, was sufficient to infuse a certain share of apprehension into the minds of the stoutest men, and it was hardly reckoned to derogate from the courage of a tried soldier that he should quail in spirit before the dreadful presence of the Powers of Darkness. Dauntrees had an undoubting faith in the malignant influences which were said to hover about the Wizard's Chapel, and nothing but the pride and subordination of his profession could have impelled him to visit this spot at an hour when its mysterious and mischievous inhabitants were supposed to be endued with their fullest power to harm. The Ranger was not less keenly impressed with the same feelings, whilst Pamesack, credulous and superstitious as all of his tribe, was, like them, endowed with that deeply-imprinted fatalism, which taught him to suppress his emotions, and which rendered him seemingly indifferent to whatever issue awaited his enterprise.

"By my troth, Arnold," said Dauntrees, as they strode forward, "although we jest at yonder white-livered vintner, this matter we have in hand might excuse an ague in a stouter man. I care not to confess that the love I bear his Lordship, together with some punctilio of duty, is the only argument that might bring me here to-night. I would rather stand a score pikes in an onset with my single hand, where the business is with flesh and blood, than buffet with a single imp of the Wizard. I have heard of over-bold men being smote by the evil eye of a beldam hag; and I once knew a man of unquenchable gaiety suddenly made mute and melancholy by the weight of a blow dealt by a hand which was not to be seen: the remainder of his life was spent in sorrowful penance. They say these spirits are quick to punish rashness."

"As Lord Charles commands we must do his bidding," replied the forester. "When the business in hand must be done, I never stop to think of the danger of it. If we should not get back, Lord Charles has as good men to fill our places. I have been scared more than once by these night devils, till my hair lifted my cap with the fright, but I never lost my wits so far as not to strike or to run at the good season."

"*Laet lopen die lopen luste,* as we used to say in Holland," returned the Captain. "I am an old rover and have had my share of goblins, and never flinched to sulphur or brimstone, whether projected by the breath of a devil or a culverin. I am not to be scared now from my duty by any of Paul Kelpy's brood, though I say again I like not this strife with shadows. His Lordship shall not say we failed in our outlook. I did purpose, before we set out, to talk with Father Pierre concerning this matter, but Garret's wine and his wife together put it out of my head."

"The holy father would only have told you," replied Arnold, "to keep a Latin prayer in your head and Master Weasel's wine and wife both out of it."

"So he would, Arnold, and it would have gone more against the grain than a hair-shirt penance. I have scarce a tag of a prayer in my memory, not even a line of the Fac Salve; and I have moreover a most special need for a flask of that vintage of Teneriffe on a chilly night;—and then, as you yourself was a witness, I had most pressing occasion to practise a deceit upon Mistress Dorothy. The Priest's counsel would have been wasted words—that's true: so we were fain to do our errand to-night without the aid of the church.—Why do you halt, Pamesack?"

"I hear the tread of a foot," replied the Indian.

"A deer stalking on the shore of the creek," said Dauntrees.

"More like the foot of a man," returned Pamesack, in a lowered voice; "we should talk less to make our way safe.—There is the growl of a dog."

Arnold now called the attention of his companions to the outlines of a low hut which was barely discernible through the wood where an open space brought the angle of the roof into relief against the water of the creek, and as they approached near enough to examine the little structure more minutely, they were saluted by the surly bark of a deep throated dog, fiercely redoubled. At the same time the sound of receding footsteps was distinctly audible.

"Who dwells here?" inquired Dauntrees, striking the door with the hilt of his sword.

There was no answer, and the door gave way to the thrust and flew wide open. The apartment was tenantless. A few coals of fire gleaming from the embers, and a low bench furnished with a blanket, rendered it obvious that this solitary abode had been but recently deserted by its possessor. A hasty survey of the hut, which was at first fiercely disputed by the dog—a cross-grained and sturdy mastiff—until a sharp blow from a staff which the forester bestowed sent him growling from the premises, satisfied the explorers that so far, at least, they had encountered nothing supernatural; and without further delay or comment upon this incident they took their course along the margin of St. Jerome's Creek. After a short interval, the beating of the waves upon the beach informed them that they had reached the neighbourhood of the shore of the Chesapeake. Here a halt and an attentive examination of the locality made them aware that they stoodu upon a bank, which descended somewhat abruptly to the level of the beach that lay some fifty yards or more beyond them. In the dim starlight they were able to trace the profile of a low but capacious tenement which stood almost on the tide mark.

"It is the Chapel!" said Dauntrees, in an involuntary whisper as he touched the Ranger's arm.

"It is Paul Kelpy's house, all the same as I have known it these twenty years:—a silent and wicked house," whispered Arnold, in reply.

"And a pretty spot for the Devil to lurk in," said Dauntrees, resuming his ordinary tone.

"Hold, Captain," interrupted the Ranger, "no foul words so near the Haunted House. The good saints be above us!" he added, crossing himself and muttering a short prayer.

"Follow me down the bank," said Dauntrees, in a low but resolute voice; "but first look to your carbines that they be charged and primed. I will break in the door of this ungodly den and ransack its corners before I leave it. Holy St. Michael, the Archfiend is in the Chapel, and warns us away!" he exclaimed, as suddenly a flash of crimson light illuminated every window of the building. "It is the same warning given to Burton and myself once before. Stand your ground, comrades; we shall be beset by these ministers of sin!"

As the flashes of this lurid light were thrice repeated, Pamesack was seen on the edge of the bank fixed like a statue, with foot and arm extended, looking with a stern gaze towards this appalling spectacle. Arnold recoiled a pace and brought his hand across his eyes, and was revealed in this posture as he exclaimed in his marked Dutch accent, "The fisherman's blood is turned to fire: we had best go no further, masters." Dauntrees had advanced half-way down the bank, and the glare disclosed him as suddenly arrested in his career; his sword gleamed above his head whilst his short cloak was drawn by the motion of his left arm under his chin; and his broad beaver, pistolled belt, and wide boots, now tinged with the preternatural light, gave to his figure that rich effect which painters are pleased to copy.

"I saw Satan's imps within the chamber," exclaimed the Captain. "As I would the blessed Martyrs be with us, I saw the very servitors of the Fiend! They are many and mischievous, and shall be defied though we battle with the Prince of the Air. What ho, bastards of Beelzebub, I defy thee! in the name of our patron, the holy and blessed St. Ignatius, I defy thee!"

There was a deeper darkness as Dauntrees rushed almost to the door of the house with his sword in his hand. Again the same deep flashes of fire illumed the windows, and two or three figures in grotesque costume, with strange unearthly faces, were seen, for the instant, within. Dauntrees retreated a few steps nearer to his companions, and drawing a pistol, held it ready for instant use. It was discharged at the windows with the next flash of the light, and the report was followed by a hoarse and yelling laugh from the tenants of the house.

"Once more I defy thee!" shouted the Captain, with a loud voice; "and in the name of our holy church, and by the order of the Lord Proprietary, I demand what do you here with these hellish rites?"

The answer was returned in a still louder laugh, and in a shot fired at the challenger, the momentary light of the explosion revealing, as Dauntrees imagined, a cloaked figure presenting a harquebuss through the window.

"Protect yourselves, friends!" he exclaimed, "with such shelter as you may find," at the same time retreating to the cover of an oak which stood upon the bank. "These demons show weapons like our own. I will e'en ply the trade with thee, accursed spirits!" he added, as he discharged a second pistol.

The Ranger and Pamesack had already taken shelter, and their carbines were also levelled and fired. Some two or three shots were returned from the house accompanied with the same rude laugh which attended the first onset, and the scene, for a moment, would have been thought rather to resemble the assault and defence of mortal foes, than the strife of men with intangible goblins, but that there were mixed with it other accompaniments altogether unlike the circumstance of mortal battle; a loud heavy sound as of rolling thunder, echoed from the interior of the chapel, and in the glimpses of light the antic figures within were discerned as dancing with strange and preposterous motions.

"It avails us not to contend against these fiends," said Dauntrees. "They are enough to maintain their post against us, even if they fought with human implements. Our task is accomplished by gaining sight of the chapel and its inmates. We may certify what we have seen to his Lordship; so, masters, move warily and quickly rearward. Ay, laugh again, you juggling minions of the devil!" he said, as a hoarse shout of exultation resounded from the house, when the assailants commenced their retreat. "Put on the shape of men and we may deal with you! Forward, Arnold; if we tarry, our retreat may be vexed with dangers against which we are not provided."

"I hope this is the last time we shall visit this devil's den," said Arnold, as he obeyed the Captain's injunction, and moved, as rapidly as his long stride would enable him to walk, from the scene of their late assault.

Whilst these events were passing, I turn back to the publican, who was left a full mile in the rear to guard the baggage and keep up the fire,—a post, as he described it, of no small danger.

It was with a mistrusting conscience, as to the propriety of his separation from his companions, that Garret, when he had leisure for reflection, set himself to scanning his deportment at this juncture. His chief scruple had reference to the point of view in which Dauntrees and Arnold de la Grange would hereafter represent this incident: would they set it down, as Weasel hoped they might, to the account of a proper and soldier-like disposition of the forces, which required a detachment to defend a weak point? or would they not attribute his hanging back to a want of courage, which his conscience whispered was not altogether so wide of the truth, but which he had hoped to conceal by his martial tone of bravado? There are many brave men, he reflected, who have a constitutional objection to fighting in the dark, and he was rather inclined to rank himself in that class. "In the dark," said he, as he sat down by the fire, with his hands locked across his knees, which were drawn up before him in grasshopper angles, and looked steadily at the blazing brushwood; "in the dark a man cannot see—that stands to reason. And it makes a great difference, let me tell you, masters, when you can't see your enemy. A brave man, by nature, requires light. And, besides, what sort of an enemy do we fight? Hobgoblins—not mortal men—for I would stand up to any mortal man in Christendom; ay, and with odds against me. I have done it before now. But these whirring and whizzing ghosts and their cronies, that fly about one's ears like cats, and purr and mew like bats—what am I saying? no, fly like bats and mew like cats—one may cut and carve at them with his blade with no more wound than a boy's wooden truncheon makes upon a south wind. Besides, the Captain, who is all in all in his command, hath set me here to watch, which, as it were, was a forbidding of me to go onward. He must be obeyed: a good soldier disputes no order, although it go against his stomach. It was the Captain's wish that I should keep strict watch and ward here on the skirt of the wood; otherwise, I should have followed him—and with stout heart and step, I warrant you! But the Captain hath a soldierly sagacity in his cautions; holding this spot, as he wisely hath done, to be an open point of danger, an inlet, as it were, to circumvent his march, and therefore straightly to be looked to. Well, let the world wag, and the upshot be what it may, here are comforts at hand, and I will not stint to use them."

Saying this the self-satisfied martialist opened the basket and solaced his appetite with a slice of pasty and a draught of wine.

"I will now perform a turn of duty," he continued, after his refreshment; and accordingly drawing his hanger, he set forth to make a short circuit into the open field. He proceeded with becoming caution on this perilous venture, looking slyly at every weed or bush which lay in his route, shuddering with a chilly fear at the sound of his own footsteps, and especially scanning, with a disturbed glance, the vibrations of his long and lean shadow which was sharply cast by the fire across the level ground. He had wandered some fifty paces into the field, on this valorous outlook, when he bethought him that he had ventured far enough, and might now return, deeming it more safe to be near the fire and the horses than out upon a lonesome plain, which he believed to be infested by witches and their kindred broods. He had scarcely set his face towards his original post when an apparition came upon his sight that filled him with horror, and caused his hair to rise like bristles. This was the real bodily form and proportions of such a spectre as might be supposed to prefer such a spot—an old woman in a loose and ragged robe, who was seen gliding up to the burning fagots with a billet of pine in her hand, which she lighted at the fire and then waved above her head as she advanced into the field towards the innkeeper. Weasel's tongue clave to the roof of his mouth, and his teeth chattered audibly against each other, his knees smote together, and his eyes glanced steadfastly upon the phantom. For a moment he lost the power of utterance or motion, and when these began to return, as the hag drew nearer, his impulse was to fly; but his bewildered reflection came to his aid and suggested greater perils in advance: he therefore stood stock-still.

"Heaven have mercy upon me!—the Lord have mercy upon me, a sinner!" he ejaculated; "I am alone, and the enemy has come upon me."

"Watcher of the night," said a voice, in a shrill note, "draw nigh. What do you seek on the wold?"

"Tetra grammaton, Ahaseel—in the name of the Holy Evangels, spare me!" muttered the innkeeper, fruitlessly ransacking his memory for some charm against witches, and stammering out an incoherent jargon. "Abracadabra—spare me, excellent and worthy dame! I seek no hurt to thee. I am old, mother, too old and with too many sins of my own to account for, to wish harm to any one, much less to the good woman of this wold. Oh Lord, oh Lord! why was I seduced upon this fool's errand?"

"Come nigh, old man, when I speak to you. Why do you loiter there?" shouted the witch, as she stood erect some twenty paces in front of the publican and beckoned him with her blazing fagot. "What dost thou mutter?"

"I but sported with my shadow, mother," replied Weasel, with a tremulous attempt at a laugh, as he approached the questioner, in an ill assumed effort at composure and cheerfulness. "I was fain to divert myself with an antic, till some friends of mine, who left me but a moment since, returned. How goes the night with you dame?"

"Merrily," replied the hag, as she set up a shrill laugh which more resembled a scream, "merrily; I cannot but laugh to find the henpecked vintner of St. Mary's at this time of night within the sound of the tide at the Black Chapel. I know your errand, old chapman of cheap liquors, and why you have brought your cronies. You pretend to be a liegeman of his Lordship, and you travel all night to cheat him of five shillings. You will lie on the morrow with as sad a face as there is in the hundred. I know you."

"You know all things, worthy dame, and I were a fool to keep a secret from you. What new commodity, honest mistress, shall I find with Rob? The port is alive with a rumour of the Olive Branch; I would be early with the Cripple. Ha, ha!" he added, with a fearful laugh, "thou seest I am stirring in my trade."

"Garret Weasel," said the beldam, "you may take it for a favour, past your deservings, that Rob will see thee alone at his hut even in day time: but it is as much as your life is worth to bring your huff-cap brawlers to St. Jerome's at midnight. It is not lawful ground for thee, much less for the hot-brained fools who bear you company. Who showed them the path to my cabin, that I must be driven out at this hour?"

"Worthy mistress, indeed I know not. I am ignorant of what you say!"

"They will call themselves friends to the Chapel: but we have no friends to the Chapel amongst living men. The Chapel belongs to the dead and the tormentors of the dead. So follow your cronies and command them back. I warn you to follow, and bring them back, as you would save them from harm. Ha! look you, it is come already!" she exclaimed, raising her torch in the air, as the flashes from the Haunted House illumined the horizon; "the seekers have roused our sentries, and there shall be angry buffets to the back of it!" At this moment the first shot was heard. "Friends, forsooth!" she shouted at the top of her voice: "friends, are ye? there is the token that ye are known to be false liars. Wo to the fool that plants his foot before the Chapel! Stand there, Garret Weasel: I must away; follow me but a step—raise thy head to look after my path, and I will strike thee blind and turn thee into a drivelling idiot for the rest of thy days. Remember——"

In uttering this threat the figure disappeared; Garret knew not how, as he strictly obeyed the parting injunction, and his horrors were greatly increased by the report of the several shots which now reached his ear from the direction of the Black House.

He had hardly recovered himself sufficiently to wander back to the fire, before Dauntrees, Arnold, and Pamesack arrived, evidently flurried by the scene through which they had passed, as well as by the rapidity of their retreat.

"Some wine, Garret! some wine, old master of the tap!" was Dauntrees' salutation; "and whilst we regale as briefly as we may, have thou our horses loose from the trees; we must mount and away. To the horses, Garret! We will help ourselves."

"I pray you, Master Captain," inquired the publican, having now regained his self-possession, "what speed at the Chapel? Oh, an we have all had a night of it! Sharp encounters all round, masters! I can tell you a tale, I warrant you."

"Stop not to prate now," interrupted Dauntrees, in a voice choked by the huge mouthful of the pasty he was devouring; "we shall discourse as we ride. That flask, Arnold, I must have another draught e'er we mount, and then, friends, to horse as quickly as you may; we may be followed; we may have ghost, devil, and man of flesh, all three, at our heels."

"I have had store of them, I can tell you—ghosts and devils without number," said Weasel, as he brought the horses forward.

"You shall be tried by an inquest of both, for your life, if you tarry another instant," interposed the Captain, as he sprang into his saddle.

"What! are we set upon, comrades?" cried out the vintner, manfully, as he rose to his horse's back, and pricked forward until he got between Pamesack and Arnold. "Are we set upon? Let us halt and give them an accolado; we are enough for them, I warrant you! Oh, but it had well nigh been a bloody night," he continued, as the whole party trotted briskly from the ground. "We had work to do, masters, and may tell of it to-morrow. Good Pamesack, take this basket from me, it impedes my motion in these bushes. Master Arnold, as we must ride here in single files, let me get before thee: I would speak with the Captain. Who should I see, Captain Dauntrees," continued the publican, after these arrangements were made, and he had thrust himself into the middle of the line of march, and all now proceeded at a slackened pace, "but that most notorious and abominable hag, the woman of Warrington—Kate, who lives, as every body knows, on the Cliffs. She must needs come trundling down before me, astride a broomstick, with a black cat upon her shoulder, and sail up to the fire which I had left, for a space, to make a round on my watch—for you may be sworn a strict watch I made of it, going even out of my way to explore the more hidden and perilous lurking-places where one might suspect an enemy to lie. So, whilst I was gone on this quest, she whips in and seats herself by the fire, with a whole score of devils at their antics around her. Then up I come, naturally surprised at this audacity, and question them, partly in soldier-wise, showing my sword ready to make good my speech, and partly by adjuration, which soon puts me the whole bevy to flight, leaving Kate of Warrington at mercy: and there I constrained her to divulge the secrets of the Chapel. She said there had been devilish work under that roof, and would be again; when pop, and bang, and slash, and crash, I heard the outbreak, and saw the devil's lights that were flashed. I could hold no longer parley with the hag, but was just moving off at full speed to your relief, determined in this need to desert my post—which, in my impatience to lend you a hand, I could not help—when I heard your footfall coming back, and so I was fain to bide your coming."

"A well conceived sally of soldiership," said Dauntrees, "and spoken with a cavalier spirit, Master Garret. It hath truth upon the face of it: I believe every word. It shall serve you a good turn with his Lordship. What does Kate of Warrington in this neighbourhood? She travels far on her broomstick—unless, indeed, what seems likely, she has taken her quarters in the cabin we disturbed to-night. These crows will be near their carrion."

By degrees the party, as they pursued their homeward journey, grew drowsy. The publican had lost all his garrulity, and nodded upon his horse. Arnold and Pamesack rode in silence, until Dauntrees, as if waking up from a reverie, said—

"Well, friends, we return from no barren mission to-night. His Lordship may have some satisfaction in our story; particularly in the vintner's. We shall be ready to report to his Lordship by noon, and after that we shall hasten to quiet our Dame Dorothy. The night is far spent: I should take it, Arnold, to be past three o'clock, by the rising of the moon. At peep of day we shall be snug upon our pallets, with no loss of relish for a sleep which will have been well earned."

As the Captain continued to urge his journey, which he did with the glee that waits upon a safe deliverance from an exploit of hazard, he turned his face upwards to the bright orb which threw a cheerful light over the scenery of the road-side, and in the distance flung a reflection, as of burnished silver, over the broad surface of St. Mary's river, as seen from the height which the travellers were now descending. Not more than two miles of their route remained to be achieved, when the Captain broke forth with an old song of that day, in a voice which would not have discredited a professor:

"The moon, the moon, the jolly moon,
And a jolly old queen is she!
She hath stroll'd o' nights this thousand year,
With ever the best of company.
Sing, Hic and hoc sumus nocturno,
Huzza for the jolly old moon!"

"Why, Garret, vintner, art asleep, man?" inquired the Captain. "Why dost thou not join in the burden?"

"To your hand, Captain," exclaimed Weasel, rousing himself and piping forth the chorus—

"Hic and hoc sumus nocturno,
Huzza for the jolly old moon!"

which he did not fail to repeat at the top of his voice at each return.

Dauntrees proceeded:

"She trails a royal following,
And a merry mad court doth keep,
With her chirping boys that walk i' the shade,
And wake when the bailiff's asleep.
Sing, Hic and hoc sumus nocturno,
Huzza for the jolly old moon!

"Master Owl he is her chancellor,
And the bat is his serving-man;
They tell no tales of what they see,
But wink when we turn up the can.
Sing, Hic and hoc sumus nocturno,
Huzza for the jolly old moon!

"Her chorister is Goodman Frog,
With a glow-worm for his link;
And all who would make court to her,
Are fain, good faith! to drink.
Sing, Hic and hoc sumus nocturno,
Huzza for the jolly old moon!"

This ditty was scarcely concluded—for it was spun out with several noisy repetitions of the chorus—before the troop reined up at the gate of the Fort. The drowsy sentinel undid the bolt at the Captain's summons, and, in a very short space, the wearied adventurers were stretched in the enjoyment of that most satisfactory of physical comforts, the deep sleep of tired men.

CHAPTER XII

There remains
A rugged trunk, dismember'd and unsightly,
Waiting the bursting of the final bolt
To splinter it to shivers.

The Doom of Devorgoil.

The shore of the Chesapeake between Cape St. Michael—as the northern headland at the mouth of Potomac was denominated by the early settlers—and the Patuxent, is generally flat, and distinguished by a clear pebbly beach or strand. The shore, comprising about twenty miles, is intersected by a single creek, that of St. Jerome, which enters the bay some five or six miles north of the Potomac. The line of beach, which I have referred to, is here and there relieved by small elevations which in any other region would scarce deserve the name, but which are sufficiently prominent in this locality to attract remark. From the general level of the country they rise high enough to afford a clear prospect over the wide waters, and no less to distinguish the landward perspective to the mariner whose eye eagerly seeks the varieties of landscape as he holds his course up the bay. At a few points these small hills terminate immediately upon the tide in the abrupt form of a cliff, and, at others, take the shape of a knoll sinking away by a rapid, but grass-covered, declivity to the strand. This latter feature is observable in the vicinity of St. Jerome's, where the slope falls somewhat abruptly to the level of the tide, leaving something above fifty paces in width of low ground between its base and the ordinary water-mark. It was upon this flat that, in ancient times, stood the dwelling house of Paul Kelpy the fisherman—a long, low building of deal boards, constructed somewhat in the shape of a warehouse or magazine. Some quarter of a mile along the beach, so sheltered under the brow of the slope as scarcely to be seen amongst the natural shrubbery that shaded it, stood a cottage or hut of very humble pretensions. It was so low that a man of ordinary height, while standing at the door, might lay his hand upon the eaves of the roof, and correspondent to its elevation, it was so scanty in space as to afford but two apartments, of which the largest was not above ten feet square. It was strongly built of hewn logs, and the door, strengthened by nails thickly studded over its surface, was further fortified by a heavy padlock, which rendered it sufficiently impregnable against a sharper assault than might be counted on from such as ordinarily should find motive to molest the proprietor of such a dwelling.

A small enclosure surrounded the hut and furnished ground for some common garden plants which were not neglected in their culture. A few acres, on the higher plain above the bank, exhibited signs of husbandry; and the small nets and other fishing tackle disposed about the curtilage, together with a skiff drawn up on the sand, gave evidence of the ostensible thrift by which the occupant of the hut obtained a livelihood.

To this spot I propose to introduce my reader, the day preceding that at which my story has been opened. It was about an hour before sunset, and a light drizzling rain, with a steady wind from the north-east, infused a chilly gloom into the air, and heightened the tone of solitude which prevailed over the scene. A thin curl of smoke which rose from the clumsy chimney of the hut gave a sign of habitation to the premises, and this was further confirmed by the presence of a large and cross-visaged mastiff-bitch, whose heavy head might be discerned thrust forth from beneath the sill of the gable,—a sullen warder of this sullen place of strength. The waves, now propelled upon a flood tide, rolled in upon the shore, and broke almost at the door of the hut, with a hoarse and harsh and ceaseless plash. Far out over the bay, the white caps of the wind-driven surge floated like changing snow drifts upon the surface of the waters. The water fowl rose in squadrons above this murky waste and struggled to windward, in a flight so low as frequently to shield them from the sight in the spray. An old bald eagle perched on the loftiest branch of a lightning-riven tree, immediately upon the bank above the hut, kept anxious watch upon her nest which, built in the highest fork, rocked to and fro in the breeze, whilst her screams of warning to her young seemed to answer to the din of the waters.

In the larger apartment of the hut a few fagots blazed upon the hearth, supplying heat to a pot that simmered above them, the care of which, together with other culinary operations, engaged the attention of a brown, haggard and weather-beaten woman, who plied this household duty with a silent and mechanical thrift. She was not the only tenant of the dwelling. Remote from the hearth, and immediately below a small window, sat, apparently upon the floor, a figure eminently calculated to challenge observation. His features were those of a man of seventy, sharp, shrewd and imprinted with a deep trace of care. His frame indicated the possession, at an earlier period of his life, of the highest degree of strength; it was broad in the shoulders, ample in chest, and still muscular, although deprived of its roundness by age. His dress, of coarse green serge, made into a doublet with skirts that fell both front and rear, secured by a leathern belt, was so contrived as to conceal, in his present posture, his lower extremities. A broad ruff received his locks of iron gray, which fell over his back in crisp wiry curls: a thick grizzly beard, of the same hue, gave an elongation to his countenance which imparted to the observer the unpleasant impression of a head disproportionally large for the body, at least as seen in its present aspect. His eyes dark and unusually clear, were sunk deep in their sockets, whilst a shaggy and matted brow, overhanging them like a porch, gave sometimes an almost preternatural brilliancy to their quick and changeful glances—like the sparkling of water when agitated in a well. It was observable from the dropping in of the upper jaw that he had lost his teeth, and this perhaps had given a tendency of the strong furrowed lines and seams, with which his features were marked, to converge towards the mouth.

His girdle sustained a long knife or dagger, which apparently constituted a part of his daily equipment; and the oblique flash of his eye, and tremulous motion of his thin lip betrayed a temperament, from which one might infer that this weapon of offence was not worn merely as an ornament of the person.

The individual described in this summary was familiar to report, throughout the province, as The Cripple. His true name was supposed to be Robert Swale,—but this was almost lost in the pervading popular designation of Rob of the Bowl, or Trencher Rob—an appellative which he had borne ever since his arrival in the province, now some fifteen years gone by. Of his history but little was known, and that little was duly mystified, in the public repute, by the common tendency in the vulgar mind to make the most of any circumstance of suspicion. The story went that he had been shipwrecked, on a winter voyage, upon this coast, and, after suffering incredible hardships, had saved his life only at the expense of the loss of both legs by frost. In this maimed condition he had reached the shore of the province, and some time afterwards built the hut in which he now dwelt, near the mouth of St. Jerome's. Here he had passed many years, without attracting other notice than such as the stinted charity of the world affords, when it is exercised upon the fate or fortunes of an obscure recluse. This observation began to find a broader scope as soon as it became obvious that the hermit was not altogether an object of almsgiving; and the little world of this part of the province discovering in process of time that he was not absolutely penniless, were fain to take offence at the mystery of his means of earning his frugal subsistence. Before many years, some few of the traders and country people round had found out that Rob was occasionally possessed of good merchantable commodities much in request by the inhabitants of the port, and dark whispers were sometimes circulated touching the manner in which he came by them. These surmises were not made topics of public discussion for two reasons;—first, because it was not inconvenient or unprofitable to the traders in the secret to deal with Rob;—and secondly, Rob was not a man to allow this indulgence of idle speculation; he was of an irascible temper, free to strike when crossed, and, what was still more to be feared, had friends who were not unwilling to take up his quarrel. The loss of his legs was supplied by a wooden bowl or trencher, of an elliptical shape, to which his thighs were attached by a strap, and this rude contrivance was swayed forward, when the owner chose, by the aid of two short crutches, which enabled him to lift himself from the ground and assume a progressive motion. It was to the exercise which this mode of locomotion imposed upon his upper limbs, that the unusual breadth and squareness of his figure about the shoulders, as well as the visible manifestations of strength of arm for which he was remarkable, were in part, perhaps, to be attributed. Use had made him expert in the management of his bowl, and he could keep pace pretty fairly with an ordinary walker. The Cripple was a man of unsocial habits and ascetic life, although there were times in which his severe temper relaxed into an approach to companionable enjoyment, and then his intercourse with the few who had access to him was marked by a sarcastic humour and keen ridicule of human action which showed some grudge against the world, and, at the same time, denoted conversancy with mankind, and by no means a deficiency of education. But, in general, his vein was peevish, and apt to vent itself in indiscriminate petulance or stern reproof.

A small painting of St. Romuald at his devotions, by the hand of Salvator himself, hung over a dressing table, in the back room of the hut in which the bed of the Cripple was placed; and this exquisite gem of art, which the possessor seemed duly to appreciate, was surmounted by a crucifix, indicating the religious faith in which he worshipped. This might be gathered also from a curious, antique pix, of heavy gilded metal, a ponderous missal with silver clasps, a few old volumes of the lives of the saints, and other furniture of the like nature, all of which denoted that the ingredient of a religious devotee formed an element in his singular compound of character.

The superiority of his mind and attainments over those of the mass of the inhabitants of the province had contributed to render the Cripple an object of some interest as well as of distrust amongst them, and this sentiment was heightened into one approaching to vulgar awe, by the reputation of the person who had always been somewhat in his confidence, and now attended him as his servitress and only domestic. This person was the ungainly and repulsive beldam whom I have already noticed as ministering in the household concerns of the hut. She was a woman who had long maintained a most unenviable fame as The Woman of Warrington, in the small hamlet of that name on the Cliffs of Patuxent, from whence she had been recently transplanted to perform the domestic drudgery in which we have found her. Her habitation was a rude hovel some few hundred paces distant from the hut of the Cripple, on the margin of St. Jerome's creek, and within gunshot of the rear of the Black Chapel. To this hovel, after her daily work was done, she retired to pass the night, leaving her master or patron to that solitude which he seemed to prefer to any society. The surly mastiff-bitch, we have noticed, alternately kept guard at the hut of the master and domestic,—roving between the two in nightly patrol, with a gruff and unsocial fidelity,—no unsuitable go-between to so strange a pair. It will not be wondered at, that, in a superstitious age, such an association as that of the Cripple and the crone, in the vicinity of such a spot, desecrated, as the Fisherman's lodge had been, by the acting of a horrible tragedy, should excite, far and wide amongst the people, a sentiment of terror sufficiently potent to turn the steps of the wayfarer, as the shades of evening fell around him, aside from the path that led to St. Jerome's.

The Cripple, at the time when I have chosen to present him to my reader, was seated, as I have said, immediately beneath the window. A pair of spectacles assisted his vision as he perused a pacquet of papers, several of which lay scattered around him. The dim light for a while perplexed his labour, and he had directed the door to be thrown wide open that he might take advantage of the last moment before the approaching twilight should arrest his occupation. Whilst thus employed, the deadened sound of a shot boomed across the bay.

"Ha!" he exclaimed as he threw aside the paper in his hand and directed his eyes towards the water; "there is a signal—by my body, a signal gun!—an ill bird is flying homeward. Did you not hear that shot, woman?"

"I had my dream of the brigantine two nights ago," replied the servitress; "and of the greedy kite that calls himself her master;—the shot must be his."

"Whose can it be else?" demanded the Cripple sharply, as he swung himself forward to the doorsill and shook his locks from his brow in the act of straining his sight across the dim surface of the bay. "Ay, ay; there it is. Hark—another shot!—that is the true pass word between us:—Dickon, sure enough!—The brigantine is in the offing. Cocklescraft is coming in with the speed of a gull. He comes full freighted—full freighted, as is his wont, with the world's plunder. What dole hath he done this flight?—what more wealthy knave than himself hath he robbed? Mischief, mischief, mischief—good store of it, I'll be sworn:—and a keener knave than himself he hath not found in his wide venture. He will be coming ashore to visit the Cripple, ha!—he shall be welcome—as he ever hath been. We are comrades,—we are cronies, and merry in our divisions—the Skipper and the Cripple!—there is concord in it—the Skipper and the Cripple—merry men both!"

These uprisings of the inner thoughts of the man were uttered in various tones—one moment scarce audible, the next with an emphatic enunciation, as if addressed to his companion in the hut,—and sometimes with the semblance of a laugh, or rather chuckle, which was wormwood in its accent, and brought the rheum from his eye down his cheek. The beldam, accustomed to this habit of self-communion in the Cripple, apparently heeded not these mutterings, until he, at length, accosted her with a command.—"Mistress Kate, double the contents of your pot;—the skipper and some of his men will be here presently, as keen and trenchant as their own cutlasses. They will be hungry, woman,—as these saltwater monsters always are for earthy provender."

"Such sharp-set cattle should bring their provender with them," replied the domestic, as she went about increasing her store of provision in compliance with her master's directions.

"Or the good red gold, or the good red gold, old jade!" interrupted the Cripple. "The skipper doth not shrink in the girdle from the disease of a lean purse, and is therefore worthy of our worshipful entertainment. So goes the world, and we will be in the fashion! Though the world's malisons drive him hither as before a tempest, yet, comes he rich in its gear; he shall have princely reception. I am king of this castle, and ordain it. Is he taking in sail?—is he seeking an anchorage? Ha, he understands his craft, and will be with us anon," he continued, as he marked the movements of the approaching vessel.

There might be dimly seen, nearly abreast of St. Jerome's, a close-reefed brig, holding her course before a fair wind directly across the bay towards the hut of the Cripple. She was, at intervals, lost to view behind the thickening haze, and as often re-appeared as she bent under the fresh north-east breeze and bounded rapidly with the waves towards the lee shore. It was after the hour of sunset when the tenants of the hut were just able to discern, in the murky gloom of the near nightfall, that she had lowered sail and swung round with her head seaward, at an anchorage some two miles out in the bay.

"Quick, Mistress Kate, and kindle some brush-wood on the shore," said the master of the hut. "It grows suddenly dark, and the boat's crew will need a signal to steer by."

The woman gathered a handful of fagots, and, kindling them into a blaze, transferred them to the beach in front of the hut, where, notwithstanding the rain, they burned with a steady light. This illumination had not subsided before the stroke of oars rose above the din of the waves; and the boat with her crew, sheeted with the broad glare of the signal-fire, suddenly appeared mounted on the surf, surrounded with foam and spray, and in the same instant was heard grating on the gravel of the beach.

Cocklescraft, with two seamen, entered the hut. The skipper was now in the prime of youthful manhood; tall, active and strong, with the free step and erect bearing that no less denoted the fearlessness of his nature than pride in the consciousness of such a quality. His face, tinged with a deep brown hue, was not unhandsome, although an expression of sensuality, to some extent, deprived it of its claim to be admired. A brilliant eye suffered the same disparagement by its over-ready defiance, which told of a temper obtrusively prone to quarrel. The whole physiognomy wanted gentleness, although a fine set of teeth, a regular profile, and a complexion which, with proper allowance for exposure to the weather, was uncommonly good, would unquestionably have won from the majority of observers the repute of a high degree of masculine beauty.

A scarlet jacket fitted close across the breast, wide breeches of ash-coloured stuff, hanging in the fashion of a kirtle or kilt to the knees, tight grey hose, accurately displaying the leg in all its fine proportions, and light shoes, furnished a costume well adapted to the lithe and sinewy figure of the wearer. A jet black and glossy moustache, and tuft below the nether lip, gave a martial aspect to his face, which had, nevertheless, the smoothness of skin of a boy. He wore in his embroidered belt, a pair of pistols richly mounted with chased silver and costly jewels, and his person was somewhat gorgeously and, in his present occupation, inappropriately ornamented with gems and chains of gold. His hair, in almost feminine luxuriance, descended in ringlets upon his neck. A large hat made of the palm leaf, broad enough to shade his face and shoulders, but ill sorted with the rest of his apparel, and was still less adapted to the season and the latitude he was in, though it threw into the general expression of his figure that trait of the swaggering companion which was, in fact, somewhat prominent in his character.

"How dost, friend Rob?" was his salutation in crossing the threshold; "how dost, Rob o' the Bowl, or Rob o' the Trencher?—bowl or trencher,—either likes me; I am sworn friend to both," he continued as he stooped and took the Cripple's hand.

"Ay, thy conscience has never stayed thee," was the Cripple's reply, as he received the skipper's grasp, "when thou wouldst put thy hand in another man's bowl or trencher,—and especially, Dickon, if they were made of gold. Thou hast an appetite for such dishes. How now! where do you come from?"

"That shall be answered variously, friend of the wooden platter. If you speak to me as Meinherr Von Cogglescraft, I am from Antwerp, master of the Olive Branch, with a comfortable cargo of Hollands, and wines French and Rhenish, old greybeard, and some solid articles of Dutch bulk. But if it be to the Caballero Don Ricardo,—le beso las manos!—I am from Tortuga and the Keys, Senor Capitan del Escalfador (there is much virtue in a painted cloth) with a choice assortment of knicknackeries, which shall set every wench in the province agog. I have rare velvets of Genoa, piled and cut in the choicest fashions: I have grograms, and stuffs, and sarsnets, with a whole inventory of woman trumpery—the very pick of a Spanish bark, bound from Naples to the islands, which was so foolish as to read my flag by its seeming, and just to drop into the Chafing-Dish when he thought he was getting a convoy to help him out of the way of the too pressing and inquisitive courtesies of certain lurking friends of ours in the Keys. I have, besides, some trinkets, which are none the worse for having been blessed by the church. You shall have a choice, Rob, to deck out your chamber with some saintly gems."

"Ha! I guessed thy deviltry, Dickon," said Rob, with a laugh which, as always happened when much moved, brought tears down his cheeks—"I guessed it when I saw thee step across the door-sill with that large and suspicious sombrero on thy head. It never came from Holland—though you would fain persuade the province folks that you trade no where else: it is of the breed of the tropics, and smells of Hispaniola and Santo Domingo."

"It is a tell-tale," replied Cocklescraft, "and should have been thrown overboard before this. Old Kate of Warrington, thy hand—and here is a hand for thee! How does the world use thee? Fairly, I hope, as you deserve? You shall have the sombrero, Kate: you can truss it up into a new fashion for a bonnet, and I have store of ribands to give thee to set it off."

"My share of this world's favour," said the crone, in acknowledgment of the skipper's bounty, "has never been more than the cast-off bravery of such as hold a high head over a wicked heart. I have ever served at the mess of the devil's bantlings. But, as the custom is, I must be civil and thankful for these blessings; and so, Master Cocklescraft, I give you thanks," she added with a courtesy, as she placed the hat upon her head and strutted fantastically in the room, "for your dainty head-gear that you are unwilling to wear, and durst not, master, before the Port Wardens of St. Mary's."

"How, Kate!" exclaimed the skipper, "you have lost no whit of that railing tongue I left with you at my last venture? I marvel that the devil hath not shorn it, out of pure envy. But I know, Kate, you can do justice to the good will of a friend, after all: I would have thee to know that thou hast not been unconsidered, good mother of a thousand devilkins: I have brought thee stuff for a new gown, rich and ladylike, Kate, and becoming thy grave and matronly years, and sundry trickeries for it, by way of garniture; and, reverend dam of night-monsters, I have in store for thee some most choice distillations of the West Indies, both plain and spiced. Thou dost not spurn the strong waters, Kate of Warrington,—nor the giver of them?"

"This is a make-peace fashion of thine," said the beldam, relaxing into a smile. "You thought not of the woman of Warrington—no, not so much as a dog's dream of her—until it chanced to come into your head that the foolish crone had a will which it might not be for your good to set against you. I knew your incoming, Richard Cocklescraft, before it was thought of in the province; and I know when your outgoing will be. You come with a surly sky and a gay brow;—you shall trip it hence with a bright heaven above you, and deftly, boy—but with a heavy heart and a new crime upon thy soul."

"Peace, woman! I will hear none of thy croakings—it is an old trick of thine; the device is too stale," said Cocklescraft, half playfully and half vexed. "You are no conjuror, Kate, as you would make the world believe by these owl-hootings: if you had but a needle's-eyeful of the true witch in you, you would have foretold what bounty my luck has brought you.—Rob, we have packages to land to-night. Is the Chapel ready for our service?"

"How should it be other than ready? Doth not the devil keep his quarters there?" said Rob with a low-toned chuckle that shook his figure for some moments, and almost closed his eyes; "hath he not his court in the Chapel? Go ask the whole country side: they will swear to it on their bible oaths. Sundries have seen the hoofs and horns, and heard the howlings,—ay, and smelt the brimstone—ha, ha, ha! They'll swear to it. Is the Chapel ready, in sooth! It is a precious Chapel! Paul Kelpy, thou wert an honest cut-throat, to bedevil so good a house: we turn it to account—ha, ha! It needs but to take the key, Dickon. I warrant you ne'er a man in the province, burgher or planter, gentle or simple, ventures near enough to molest you."

"The surf runs high," said Cocklescraft, "and may give us trouble in the landing to-night; and as daylight must not find me in this latitude, I shall put what I may ashore before the dawn, and then take a flight to the opposite side of the bay. To-morrow night I shall finish my work; and you shall soon after hear, at St. Mary's, that the good and peaceful brigantine, the Olive Branch, has arrived from Holland. Meantime, I will leave you a half dozen men to garrison the Chapel, Rob."

"It is so well garrisoned with my merry goblins already," said Rob, "that it requires but a light watch. The fires alone would frighten his Lordship's whole array of rangers. That was a pretty device of mine, Dickon—blue, green, and red—excellent devil-fires all! Then I have masks—faith, most special masks! the very noses of them would frighten the short-winded train-bands of the Port into catalepsy. And the Chapel had an ill name when the fisherman shed blood on the floor: but since we blackened it, Richard—oh, that was a subtle thought!—it is past all power of exorcism: there is an ague in the very name of the Black Chapel." And here the Cripple gave way to a burst of laughter, which had been struggling for vent during all this reference to the arts by which he had contrived to maintain the popular dread of the fisherman's lodge.

Whilst this conference was held, the crone had prepared their evening meal, which being now ready, Rob was lifted upon a low platform that brought him to the proper level with the table, where he was able to help himself. Cocklescraft partook with him, and might almost have envied the keen gust and ravenous appetite with which his host despatched the coarse but savoury fare of the board—for the Cripple's power of stomach seemed to be no whit impaired by age. He continued to talk, during his meal, in the same strain which we have described, now indulging a peevish self-communion, now bursting forth with some sarcastic objurgation of the world, and again breaking a jest with his visiter.

When the seamen, under the ministration of the aged domestic, had got their supper, Cocklescraft took his departure.

All night long lights were gleaming in the Chapel; the rain continued in a steady misty drizzle, and not a star was seen to tempt a wanderer abroad. The morning, which broke upon an atmosphere purged of its vapours, showed no trace of the brig in the vicinity of St. Jerome's. Far down the bay, hugging the eastern shore, might have been discerned what a practised mariner would affirm to be a sail; but whether ship or brig—whether outward or homeward bound, might not be told without the aid of a glass.

CHAPTER XIII

Up she rose, and forth she goes,—.
I'll mote she speed therefor.
Adam Bell.

Bell, my wife, she loves not strife,
Yet she will lead me if she can;
And oft, to live a quiet life,
I'm forced to yield, though I'm goodman.
It's not for a man a woman to threape,
Unless he first give o'er his plea;
As we began we now will leave
And I'll take my old cloak about me.
Old Song.

It was nine o'clock of the morning before Dauntrees and his companions, Garret and Arnold, rose from their beds. Pamesack, whose taciturnity was not greater than his indifference to fatigue, had, at an earlier hour, gone his way. A breakfast was provided in the Captain's quarters, and the three heroes of the past night sat down to it with a relish which showed that, however unfit they might be to contend against spiritual foes, their talents for this encounter of material existences were highly respectable.

"You have had a busy time of it in dreams, Master Weasel," said Dauntrees, since you laid yourself down on your truckle bed this morning. You have been re-acting your exploits at the Chapel. I heard you at daylight crying aloud for sword and dagger."

"I warrant you, Captain Dauntrees," replied the publican, "my head has been full of fantasies since I laid me down to rest—for I was exceeding weary—and weariness doth set the brain to ramble in sleep. There was good argument, too, in our deeds at St. Jerome's for a world of dreaming."

"Ah, the night has made a man of you, my gallant vintner. You should bless your stars that you fell into such worthy company. You knew not heretofore—even with your experience at Worcester—what elements of valour it pleased Heaven to mix up in the mould whereof thou wert made. A man never sufficiently values himself until he has had some such passage as this."

"Ay, and look you, Captain Dauntrees," said Garret, his eye flashing with self-gratulation, "you will reflect that I had the brunt of it *alone*, whilst you three were banded together for common defence and support. There I was, by my single self, in the very centre of them. A man needs more comfort and companionship in a matter with witches and devils, than he does against your sword and buckler fellows. Tut! I wouldn't have cared a fig for a foe that could be struck at; but these pestilent things of the dark—hags on besoms, and flying bats as big as a man, great sword-fishes walking on legs, with their screechings, and mopings, and mewings—Lord, Lord, how it tries the reins of a solitary man! But you had flashing and firing, and charging, Captain, which is more in the way of what one expects in a fight, and one is prepared for: it has life in it."

"That is most true, doughty Garret. A culverin is but the whiff of an oaten pipe, compared with a hag upon her broomstick. Thou wert ever the man to encounter these women. It needs thy mettle to face them. Now there is thy wife, Master Weasel—oh, but that is a perilous venture in store for thee! You shall go to her and have it over, whilst I make my report to his Lordship; when that is done I will straight for the Crow and Archer, to help you in the battle, which by that time will doubtless find you sore at need."

"I must go to his Lordship with you," replied Garret, in a lowered key; "I must have my hand in the report; after that we will set out together for the inn."

"Why, man!" exclaimed Dauntrees, with affected astonishment, "would you tarry to do your duty to Mistress Dorothy? Do you not know that she hath suffered agony of mind the live-long night in your behalf, and that she is now in the very tempest of her affection waiting for you?"

"I know it, I know it, worthy Captain; but it doth not become my respect for Lord Charles's service to defer his business for mine own."

"Thou shalt not budge an inch," said Dauntrees, "on any other path than that which takes thee quickly to thy loving wife."

"Truly, Captain," replied Weasel, in a dolorous tone, "I would have thee to go with me; I beseech you heartily, allow me to bear you company to his Lordship. His Lordship will think it strange I did not come: and it will take more than me to pacify the dame."

"Well, friend Weasel, in consideration that you contended single handed last night with a whole score of devils, and bore thee gallantly;

and, moreover, as it is such heavy odds against thee in this matter of Dame Dorothy—for, of a verity, I know she is in a devil of a passion at thy contumacy, and not less at mine, I'll be sworn—why we will make a muster of it and breathe our defence in solid column. Arnold will go with us. And mark me, Vintner, at the fitting time, we shall regale."

"On the best in cellar or larder at the Crow and Archer," replied Garret. "You have the word of a man and a soldier for it."

"I wot of a woman and no soldier, whose word would go further to that bargain, Garret, than yours. Make ready, friends, we must move."

Dauntrees now set his beaver jauntily over his brow, and throwing his short cloak across his arm, marched through the postern of the fort, followed by his trusty allies, to the mansion of the Lord Proprietor.

Lord Baltimore received them in his library, and there heard from the Captain a circumstantial narrative of the events of the preceding night.

"It is a strange tale," he said, "and may well perplex the faith of the simple rustics of the province. That evil spirits preside over that blood-stained house, from your testimony, Captain Dauntrees, may no longer be denied. Friends, you all saw these things?"

"All," said Garret Weasel, with emphatic solemnity as he straitened his body even beyond the perpendicular line. "Pamesack and Arnold stood by the Captain and can vouch for him. I maintained a post of danger, an please your Lordship, alone; what I saw neither the Captain, Arnold, nor Pamesack, saw—it was a fearful sight."

"What was it?" inquired the Proprietary, with some earnestness.

"A woman," replied Garret, "*seemingly* a woman, an your Lordship comprehends: but in truth a witch, as we all do know:—Kate of Warrington, of whom your Lordship has heard. She it was who came suddenly down upon the wold. How she came," here Garret shook his head, "and what came with her,—it was a sight to look upon!"

"The vintner affirms to sundry fantastic shapes of imps and spectres in company with the woman of Warrington," said Dauntrees. "We saw nothing of the hag, having left Master Weasel, some distance in our rear when we visited the Chapel. He was cold, and required comfort. What he recounts, my Lord, you have his own avouch for."

"And what say you, Arnold?" inquired his Lordship, smiling.

"These ghosts and goblins keep a hot house, and the less we have to do with them the better," replied the forester, gravely.

"They fired upon you, Captain?" said the Proprietary; "with what weapons?"

"They had the sharp crack of the musket and pistol," replied Dauntrees, "or what seemed to be such: yet I would not swear I saw carnal weapons in the strife, though in the flash I thought I noted fire arms. This may tell better than guess of mine, my Lord," he added, as he held up his cloak and pointed to a rent in one of its folds; "this hole was made by some missive from the house: whether it be a bullet mark or an elf-shot, I will not say."

"Body o' me!" exclaimed Garret Weasel, as the Captain pointed to the damage he had sustained, "I knew not this before. There was hot work, I warrant."

"There is knavery in alliance with this sorcery," said the Proprietary, as he examined the cloak. "These wicked spirits ever find kindred amongst men. They have profligate companions of flesh to profit by their devilish arts. I thank you, friends, kindly, for this venture, and will turn it to wholesome account hereafter. Fare you well."

The party left the room, and now shaping their course towards the Crow and Archer, soon descended below the bank and took the road along the beach.

Whilst they trudged through the sand and gravel, midway between the fort and the town, Dauntrees, looking behind, saw a figure descending on horseback from the main gate of the fort down to the road upon which they now travelled. It was that of a woman, whose gestures, at the distance of half a mile, were sufficiently observable to show that she urged her horse forward with impatient earnestness. As soon as she arrived at the level of the beach, her speed was increased nearly to the utmost of the faculty of the animal which bore her, and she now came flying over the sand, with her garments and loose tresses floating in the wind.

"In the devil's name, what have we here?" exclaimed Dauntrees. "As I live, it is our queen of the hostel! Oh, Garret, Garret, here is a volcano! Here is an out-come with a conclusion at hand! Stand, masters, firmly on your legs, and brace up for the onset!"

"Alack, alack!" groaned the publican; "the woman is bereft. She hath my nag from the fort."

"Ay, and rides upon your saddle, as if it were made for her," ejaculated the Captain. "Take post behind me, Garret: I will answer her speech."

"It were no more than the luck she deserves," said Garret, pettishly, "if she should fall from the nag and break her little finger, or at the least sprain an ancle-joint."

"Hold, runagates! varlets! out upon you for a filthy Captain!" shouted the dame, in a shrill voice, as she came within call of the party, and now galloped up to the spot at which they had halted. "Give me that idiot from your beastly company. Garret Weasel, Garret Weasel! you have been the death of me!"

"Good lack, Mistress Dorothy, wife, why dost thou bear thyself in such a sort as this?"

"I will bare thee to the buff, driveller, for this. Are you not steeped in wickedness and abomination by evil-consorting with this copper Captain, and this most horrid wood ranger? Hast no eye for thy family; no regard for good name, that you must be strolling o' nights with every pot-guzzler and foul-breathed and cankered cast-off of the wars? I am ashamed of thee. You have been in your cups, I warrant, the live-long night."

"Dame, I must speak, now," said Dauntrees.

"Thou, thou!" interrupted the hostess, with her face scarlet from anger. "Never in a Christian land should such as thou be permitted to lift thy head before honest people. His Lordship would do but justice to the province to chain thee up in a dark stable, as a bull which may not be trusted at large. Did you not beguile me last night with a base lie? Did you not practice upon me, you faithless, false-hearted coward?" here tears fell from the flashing eyes of the voluble landlady. "Did you not steal that lob, my husband, from me, thief?"

"Appearances, dame," replied the Captain, with a grave composure, "if they might be trusted, were certainly to my disfavour last night. But then, I knew that when this matter was all over, I had a most sufficient and excellent reason, which a considerate, virtuous, and tender-hearted woman like yourself would fully approve, when she came to hear it. There was matter in hand of great import and urgency; no revelling, dame—no riot—but brave service, enjoined by his Lordship, and which it was his Lordship's most earnest desire should be committed in part to thy husband. It was an action of pith and bravery he had on hand; and his Lordship being well aware, dame, that Garret's wife was a woman of a loving heart, and gentle withal in her nature, and not fitted to endure the wringing of her affection by such a trial as the adventure imposed upon Garret, he charged me to make some light pretext for withdrawing thy husband from thine eye, which, by fraud, I confess, I did, and am now—since Garret hath worthily achieved his most perilous duty—here to avow my own treachery. There is promotion and great advantage at hand for this which will set up thy head, dame, the highest amongst them that wear hoods."

"We have barely escaped with our lives, Mistress Dorothy," said Weasel, in a whining accent of deprecation; "we should be made much of and praised for our duty, not be set upon with taunts and foul rebukes; and when you know all, wife, you will be sorry for this wounding of our good name."

"This is but another trick," said the landlady.

"Nay, good mistress," interrupted the Captain, "I will agree to be gibbeted by thine own fair hand, if I do not satisfy thee that in this adventure we are deserving of all applause. The Lieutenant at the fort, doubtless, told thee that we were absent last night on special duty at his Lordship's command?"

"The varlet did feign such a story, when I thought to catch this fool in thy company. And he would deny me, too, the nag; but I brought such coil about his ears that he was glad to give me the beast and set all gates open. Where do you say you have spent the night?"

"At the Black Chapel, mistress," said Weasel, with a most portentous solemnity of speech: "at the Black Chapel, by his Lordship's order; and, oh, the sights we have seen! and the time we have had of it, wife! it would make thy blood freeze to hear it."

"On the honour of a soldier, dame! by the faith of this right hand!" said Dauntrees, as he offered it to the hostess and took hers, "I swear this is true. We have had a night of wonders, which you shall hear in full when the time suits. We are on our way now to the Crow and Archer, for thine especial gratification."

"Can this be true, Arnold?" inquired the mollified and bewildered landlady. "I will believe what you say."

"You may trust in every word of it, as I am a Christian man. There be marvellous doings at the Black Chapel. We have seen spirits and devils in company."

"It is graver matter, wife, than you wot of," said Weasel.

"Ride forward, dame," added Dauntrees; "you shall see us soon at the hostel. And I promise you shall have the story, too, of the Mercer's Wife from beginning to end: you shall dame."

"You are a wheedling, cogging cheat, Captain; thy roguery will have a melancholy end yet," replied the dame, as she now rode forward with a sunshiny smile playing upon features which but a few moments before were dark with storm.

When they reached the Crow and Archer they found a group of traders assembled on the quay, gazing with a busy speculation towards the mouth of the river. By degrees the crowd increased, and the rumour soon spread abroad that the Olive Branch was in sight. A vessel was, indeed, discernible across the long flat of St. Inigoe's, just entering the river, and those who professed a knowledge of nautical affairs had no scruple in announcing her as the brigantine of Cocklescraft. She was apparently an active craft, belonging to the smaller class of sea-vessels, and manifestly a faster sailer than was ordinarily to be seen at that period. A fair and fresh breeze impelled her steadily towards her haven, and as she bounded over the glittering waters, the good folks of the little city were seen clustering in knots on every prominent cliff along the high bank, and counting the minutes which brought this messenger from the old world nearer to their salutation.

Meantime the Olive Branch began to show the sparkling foam which broke upon her bow; then to give forth voices from her deck, audible to the crowd; presently to lower sail; and at last, being stripped to her bare poles and naked rigging, she glided with lessening speed, slower and slower, until her extended cable showed that her anchor was dropt and her voyage at an end.

It was past noon when the brig came to her mooring, opposite the Town House wharf, and after a brief interval, Cocklescraft, arrayed as we have before seen him, except that he had changed his sombrero for a tasseled cap of cloth, landed on the quay, and soon became the lion of the Crow and Archer.

CHAPTER XIV

Every white will have its black,
And every sweet its sour.

Old Ballad.

The birth-day festival at the Rose Croft might be said appropriately to belong to the eminent dominion of the Lady Maria. It therefore lacked nothing of her zealous supervision. With the aid of father Pierre and some female auxiliaries she had persuaded the Collector—a task of no great difficulty—to sanction the proceeding, and she was now intent upon the due ordering and setting out of the preparations. The day was still a week off when, early after breakfast, on a pleasant morning the business-fraught lady was seen in the hall, arrayed in riding hood and mantle, ready to mount a quiet black-and-white pony that, in the charge of a groom, awaited her pleasure at the door. Natta, the little Indian girl, stood by entrusted with the care of a work-bag or wallet apparently well stuffed with the materials for future occupation,—the parcel-fragments which thrifty housewives and idleness-hating dames, down to this day, are accustomed to carry with them, for the sake of the appearance, at least, of industry. Just at this moment the Proprietary came into the hall, and seeing that his worthy sister was bound on some enterprise of more than usual earnestness, he added to his customary morning salutation a playful inquiry into the purport of her excursion.

"Ah, Charles," she replied, "there are doings in the province which are above the rule of your burgesses and councils. I hold a convocation at the Rose Croft to-day, touching matters more earnest than your state affairs. We have a merry-making in the wind, and I am looked to both for countenance and advice. It is my prerogative, brother, to be mistress of all revels."

"God bless thine age, Maria!" was the affectionate reply of the Proprietary—"it wears a pleasant verdure and betokens a life of innocent thoughts and kind actions. May the saints bear thee gently onward to thy rest! Come, I will serve as your cavalier, and help you to your horse, sister.—See now, my arm has pith in it. Hither, Natta—there is the wench on the pillion—who could serve thee with a better grace than that?"

"Thanks—thanks, good brother!" ejaculated the lady as the Proprietary lifted her to her seat, and then swung the Indian girl upon the pillion behind her. "Your arm is a valiant arm, and is blessed by more than one in this province. It has ever been stretched forth in acts of charity and protection."

"Nay, Maria, you are too old to flatter. Fie! I have no advancement to offer thee. In truth thou art sovereign here—though you go through your realm with but scant attendance for one so magnified. Why is not Albert in your train? I may well spare him—as he has a liking for such service."

"Brother, I would not tax the Secretary. He hath a free foot for his own pleasure; and, methinks, he finds his way to the Rose Croft easily enough without my teaching. It is an ancient caution of mine, in such affairs, neither to mar nor make."

"Heaven help thee for a considerate spinster!" said the Proprietary with a benignant smile as he raised his hands and shook them sportively towards his sister. "Go thy ways, with thy whimsies and thy scruples;—and a blessing on them! I wish yours were our only cares:—but go thy ways, girl!" he added, as the lady set forth on her journey, and he withdrew from the door.

At the Rose Croft, the approaching merry-making had superseded all other family topics, both in parlour and kitchen. The larder was already beginning to exhibit the plentiful accumulations which, in a place of strength, might portend a siege: the stable boys were ever on the alert, with their cavalry, to do rapid errands to the town, and Michael Mossbank, the gardener, was seen in frequent and earnest consultation with John Pouch, a river-side cotter, touching supplies of fish and wild fowl.

Whilst the elder sister Alice despatched the graver duties of the housekeeping, she had consigned to Blanche the not less important care of summoning the guests, and the maiden was now seated at the table with pen in hand registering the names of those who had been, or were to be invited to the feast,—or in other words making a census of pretty nearly the whole tithable population of St. Mary's and its dependencies.

"A plague upon it for a weary labour!" she exclaimed as she threw down the pen and rested her chin upon the palm of her hand. "I know I shall forget somebody I ought not to forget—and shall be well rated for it. And then again I shall be chid for being too free with my fellowship.—What a world of names is here! I did not think the whole province had so many. There is Winnefred Hay, the Viewer's sister,—they have tales about her which, if they be true, it is not fit she should be a crony of mine—and yet I don't believe them, though many do.—Truly the Viewer will be in a grand passion if I slight her! Sister Alice, give me your advice."

"Bid her to the feast, Blanche. We should be slow to believe these rumours to the injury of a neighbour. Winnefred Hay, is not over discreet—and gives more semblance to an evil opinion than, in truth, her faults deserve: but the townspeople are scarce better in this quickness to censure—especially such as look to the tobacco viewing. Lawrence Hay's place has something to do with that scandal."

"I am glad, sister Alice, you give me an argument to indulge my own secret wish," replied Blanche; "for I like not to believe harsh reports against any of our province. And so, that is at an end. Alack!—here is another matter for counsel: Grace Blackiston says Helen Clements is too young to be at my gathering:—she has two years before her yet at school, and has only begun embroidering. Oh, but I would as soon do a barefoot penance for a month as disappoint her!—she is the wildest of all for a dance, and looks for it, I know,—though she says never a word, and has her eyes on the ground when we talk about it.—Ha, let Grace Blackiston prate as she will, Helen shall be here! Fairly, my gossip,—I will be mistress in my own house, I promise you!"

"There is room for all thy friends, young and old," said Alice; "and you should not stint to ask them for the difference of a span or so in height. You are not quite a woman yourself, Blanche,—no, nor Grace neither—although you perk yourselves up so daintily."

"Would you have the gauger's wife, sister?" inquired Blanche, with a face of renewed perplexity. "I think my dear Lady Maria would be pleased if I bid the dame—for the gauger is a good friend of his Lordship—hot-headed, they say, but that does not make him the worse—and his dame takes it kindly to be noticed."

"Even as you will, Blanche,—it is a mark of gentle nurture not to be too scrupulous with thy questions of quality—a kind neighbour will never disgrace your courtesy. But one thing, child, your father will look to:—see that you avoid these Coodes and Fendalls and even the Chiseldines. There is a feud between them and the Proprietary,—and my Lord's friends are warm in the matter,—your father amongst the rest."

"I warrant you they get no bid from me," said Blanche, as the colour mantled in her cheek. "I hate them stock and branch—yes, as my good lady hates them."

Blanche had scarcely uttered these words before the good lady herself rode past the window. The maiden bounded forth to receive her, and Alice with less precipitation followed.

"I come with pony and pillion," said the visiter as she was assisted to the ground, and bustled into the parlour. "I could not rest until I saw Blanche, to know if all her biddings were abroad. My pretty bird, pray look you to your task—you have no time to lose: there are the families beyond Patuxent—and our friends across the bay,—besides many at home that I know have not heard from you yet. And here, sweet, I have brought you some trinketry which you shall wear at the feast: a part is for Grace Blackiston, and a part for you. Thou shalt have the choice, Blanche:—but whisht!—not a word of it to Grace, because I think she hath a conceit to be jealous of thy favour."

Whilst the two sisters welcomed the lady and responded to her voluble communications in a tone of affectionate intimacy, the contents of the work-bag were thrown open to view, and successively gave rise to sundry discussions relating not only to the objects presented, but also collaterally to the thousand matters of detail connected with the festival, thus engrossing the first hour of their interview, until the subject was changed by an exclamation from Blanche, as she looked through the window upon the river—

"Oh, but here is a gallant sight!—see yonder hawk following a heron. He will strike presently—the heron cannot get away. Poor bird! how he doubles and drops in his flight to escape the swift hawk;—but it is of no avail. I should almost say it was sinful,—if it was not approved and followed by those I love best—I should hold it sinful to frighten and torture a harmless heron by such pursuit. There, the hawk has struck, and down comes hawk and quarry to the water."

"It is his Lordship's hawk," said the Lady Maria, as she looked out upon the river. "Derrick the falconer must be abroad to-day with his birds:—and now whilst I speak, there he is walking along the beach. And he is not alone neither:—by that short mantle and that feather, Blanche, you may know a friend."

The colour rose on the maiden's cheek as she said, "it is Albert, his Lordship's secretary."

"His eyes are turned this way," said the sister of the Proprietary. "A wager he comes to the house in the next ten minutes!—He would fain find some business with the Collector—I know Master Albert's occasions: nay, do not flurry thyself, my sweet Blanche."

"I wish the Secretary *would* come," returned the maiden; "we have need of him; he promised to show me how I were best to arrange my flower vases."

"Then thou shouldst do well to despatch a messenger to him," interrupted the Lady Maria, playfully; "dost thou not think he might forget?"

"Oh no, my dear lady," replied Blanche, "Master Albert never forgets a promise to me."

"Indeed! Well, I should have thought that having occasion to make you so many promises—for he is here at the Rose Croft thrice a week at least—and every visit has its promise, or I mistake—he would forget full one half."

"I deal but scantily in promises with the Secretary," replied Blanche. "Master Albert's errands here are for pastime mostly."

"Ah, he doth not forget," exclaimed the Lady Maria; "for there I see the feather of his bonnet as he climbs up the bank,—and now we have his head and shoulders; we shall get the whole man anon,—and Master Benedict Leonard in the bargain, for I see *him* trudging in the Secretary's footsteps, as he is wont to do; his young Lordship hath become the Secretary's shadow. And there is Derrick behind. They are all bound for this haven."

As the lady spoke, the Secretary was seen from the window with the heir apparent and the falconer on the verge of the bank which they had just ascended. Benedict Leonard had a hooded hawk upon his fist; and Derrick, waving a light rod to which a small streamer or flag was attached, was busy in luring down the bird that had just flown at the heron. Whilst the falconer continued his occupation the Secretary and his young companion entered the mansion.

Albert Verheyden's accost to the ladies was characterized by a familiarity not unmixed with diffidence, and a momentary flush passed, across his cheek as, after saluting Mistress Alice, and turning to Blanche, his eye fell upon the sister of the Proprietary. "I did not expect to find my honoured lady so early at the Rose Croft," he said with a profound reverence. "It should have been my duty, madam, to attend you, but I knew not of your purpose; and the falconer being bent to fly the cast of lanerets which Colonel Talbot lately sent to my Lord, would have me witness the trial, and so I came with Master Benedict to see this sport."

"Nay, Albert," replied the lady, "you should not have been of my company even if you had sought permission. I come to-day on no idle errand which might allow your loitering paces and customary delays to gaze on headlands and meadows, whereby you are wont to interrupt the course of your journey. The matter of our present meeting has need of stirring feet, which go direct to their work,—yours are not such. Still, Master Albert, you shall not be useless to-day:—here is occupation to thy hand; Blanche is in much want of a penman, and as you are of the writing craft, she would gladly enlist thee in her service—that is, if thou hast not been already marshaled and sworn under her colours."

"Master Albert, our dear lady does but jest," said Blanche. "She knows I had at first no need of better penman than myself, and now have need of none,—for, in truth, my work was finished ere she came. But your service I may command in a better task. You did promise to bring me some device for my flower-stands."

"The joiner will have them here to-day," replied the Secretary. "I have not failed to spur his industry as well as my own poor invention to that endeavour."

"Then all is done but the rendering of thanks," said Blanche, "which yet I am not in the humour to do, having matter of quarrel with you for that following of the poor heron which, but now, we saw the hawk strike down, whilst you were a looker-on, and, as we suspect, an encourager of the trespass. It was a cruel thing to assail the innocent fowl, which, being native here, has ever found friends in our house;—yes, and has daily fed upon the flat below the garden. These herons scarce fly when I walk by them on the beach. I wish the falconer had sought his quarry elsewhere than amongst my harmless birds. You should have controlled him."

"I am deeply grieved," replied the Secretary. "Indeed, I knew not of the bird nor whence he came: nor thought of it, in truth. A feather of his wing should not have come to harm had I been aware that he had ever pleased your eye. I am all unskilled in these out-door sports, and have scarce worn out the complexion of my school at Antwerp, where worldly pastimes were a forbidden thought. A poor scholar of the cloister might go free of blame if, in this sunny and gallant world, the transport of a noble game should rob him of his circumspection. I thought of naught but the glorious circling of the hawk and his swift and imperious assault. I crave your pardon for my inconsiderate error."

"You speak more like a practised cavalier than a scholar of the cloister," said the sister of the Proprietary; "thou hast a cavalier's love of the sport, Albert."

"It doth not beseem me, madam," was the Secretary's reply, "to affect a pastime which belongs neither to my rank nor humble means; but, in sadness, dear lady, I do love hawk, and hound, and steed. And when in my sequestered study—where, being, as I thought, destined to the service of the altar, I read mostly of holy men and holy things, little dreaming that I should ever see the world—it sometimes chanced, in my stray reading, I fell upon a lay wherein deeds of chivalry were told; and then I was conscious of a wish,

I am now almost ashamed to confess, that fortune might some day bring me better acquainted with that world to which such deeds belonged. Oh, blessed chance! it hath befallen now:— —that is,—I mean to say," continued the Secretary, checking himself, as his flashing eye fell to the floor, and a blush flitted across his brow—"it hath pleased Heaven to give me a kind master in my good Lord, who doth not deny me to look on when these sports are afield."

"And if we did strike down the heron, Blanche Warden," said Benedict Leonard, saucily accosting the maiden, and showing the hawk that was bound to his wrist—"what is a heron good for, but to be brought down? Herons were made for hawks—yes, and for the hawks of the Proprietary above all others; for I have heard say that every heron on the Chesapeake, within my father's boundary, is his own bird: so Derrick has said a hundred times. And there's my uncle Talbot, who flies a hawk better than any other in the province—I don't care if Derrick hears me—and has the best mews,—he says that these fire-arms have broken up hawking in the old country; and he told me I must not let it fall through when I come to the province; for my father, he thinks, doesn't care much for it. I promise you in my time we shall have hawking enough—chide as you like, Mistress Blanche. It was partly for me that my uncle Talbot sent us this cast of birds. Look at that laneret, Blanche,—look at her! Isn't that a bird? Talk to me of a goshawk after that!"

"Benedict—nephew," interposed the Lady Maria, "why dost thou fling thy bird so rudely? She brushes Blanche's cheek with her wing. Pray, not so bold: Blanche will not like thee for it."

"Blanche will never quarrel with me for loving my hawk, aunt," replied the boy playfully. "Will you, mistress? A laneret's wing and Blanche Warden's cheek are both accounted beautiful in this province, and will not grow angry with each other upon acquaintance."

"I know not that, Benedict," replied the maiden; "my cheek may grow jealous of your praise of the wing, and mischief might follow. She is but a savage bird, and hath a vicious appetite."

"I will away to the falconer," said the boy. "It is but wasting good things to talk with women about hawks. You will find me, Master Albert, along the bank with Derrick, if you have need of me."

"That boy hath more of the Talbot in him than the Calvert," said the Lady Maria, after he had left the room. "His father was ever grave from youth upwards, and cared but little for these exercises. Benedict Leonard lives in the open air, and has a light heart.—Thou hast a book under thy mantle, Master Albert," continued the lady. "Is your breviary needful when you go forth to practise a laneret?"

"It is a volume I have brought for Mistress Blanche," replied the Secretary, as, with some evident confusion, he produced a gilded quarto with clasps, from beneath his dress. "It is a delightful history of a brave cavalier, that I thought would please her."

"Ah!" exclaimed the sister of the Proprietary, taking the book and reading the title-page—"'*La très joyeuse et plaisante Histoire, composéc par le Loyal Serviteur, des faits, gestes et prouesses du bon Chevalier sans peur et sans reproche.*' Ay, and a right pleasant history it is, this of the good Knight Bayard, without fear and without reproach. But, Albert, thou knowest Blanche doth not read French."

"I designed to render it myself to Mistress Blanche, in her native tongue," replied the Secretary.

"Blanche," said the lady, shaking her head, "this comes of not taking my counsel to learn this language of chivalry long ago. See what peril you will suffer now in journeying through this huge book alone with Master Albert."

"I see no peril," replied the maiden, unconscious of the raillery. "Master Albert will teach me, ere he be done, to read French for myself."

"When thou hast such a master, and the Secretary such a pupil," said the lady, smiling, "Heaven speed us! I will eat all the French thou learnest in a month. But, Master Albert, if Blanche cannot understand your legend, in the tongue in which it is writ, she can fully comprehend your music—and so can we. It is parcel of your duty at the Rose Croft to do minstrel's service. You have so many songs—and I saw thee stealing a glance at yon lute, as if thou wouldst greet an old acquaintance."

"If it were not for Master Albert," said Alice, "Blanche's lute would be unstrung. She scarce keeps it, one would think, but for the Secretary's occupation."

"Ah, sister Alice, and my dear lady," said Blanche, "the Secretary hath such a touch of the lute, that I but shame my own ears to play upon it, after hearing his ditties. Sing, Master Albert, I pray you," she added, as she presented him the instrument.

"I will sing to the best of my skill," replied Albert, "which has been magnified beyond my deservings. With your leave, I will try a canzonet I learned in London. It was much liked by the gallants there, and I confess a favour for it because it hath a stirring relish. It runs thus:

> 'Tell me not, sweet, I am unkind,
>
> That from the nunnery

Of thy chaste breast and quiet mind
To war and arms I fly.

'True, a new mistress, now I chase,
The first foe in the field;
And with a stronger faith embrace
A sword, a horse, a shield.

'Yet this inconstancy is such
As you too shall adore:
I could not love thee, dear, so much,
Lov'd I not honour more.'"

"Well done! Well touched lute—well trolled ditty! Brave song for a bird of thy feather, Master Verheyden!" exclaimed the Collector, who, when the song was finished, entered the room with Cocklescraft. "That's as good a song, Master Cocklescraft——the Skipper, ladies—my friend of the Olive Branch, who has been with me this hour past docketing his cargo: I may call him especially your friend—he is no enemy to the vanities of this world. Ha, Master Cocklescraft, thou hast wherewith to win a world of grace with the petticoats!—thou hast an eye for the trickery of the sex! Sit down, sir—I pray you, without further reverence, sit down."

The Skipper, during this introduction, stood near the door, bowing to the company, and then advanced into the room with a careless and somewhat over-bold step, such as denotes a man who, in the endeavour to appear at his ease in society, carries his acting to the point of familiarity. Still his freedom was not without grace, and his demeanour, very soon after the slight perturbation of his first accost, became natural and appropriate to his character.

"Save you, madam," he said, addressing the sister of the Proprietary, and bowing low, "and you, Mistress Alice, and you, my young lady of the Rose Croft. It is a twelvemonth since I left the Port, and I am right glad to meet the worshipful ladies of the province once again, and to see that good friends thrive. The salt water whets a sailor's eye for friendly faces. Mistress Blanche, I would take upon me to say, without being thought too free, that you have grown some trifle taller than before I sailed. I did not then think you could be bettered in figure."

The maiden bowed without answering the Skipper's compliment.

"Richard Cocklescraft," said the Collector, "I know not if you ever saw Albert Verheyden. Had he come hither before you sailed? His Lordship's secretary."

"I was not so lucky as to fall into his company," replied Cocklescraft, turning towards the Secretary, and eyeing him from head to foot. "I think I heard that his Lordship brought new comers with him. We shall not lack acquaintance. Your hand, Master Verdun—I think so you said?" he added, as he looked inquiringly at the Collector.

The Collector again pronounced the name of the Secretary with more precision.

"Nearly the same thing," continued the Skipper. "Master Verheyden, your hand: mine is something rougher, but it shall be the hand of a comrade, if thine be in the service of worshipful Master Anthony Warden, the good Collector of St. Mary's. I know how to value a friend, Master Secretary, and a friend's friend. You have a rare voice for a ballad—I pretend to have an opinion in such matters—an excellent voice and a free finger for the lute."

"I am flattered by your liking sir," returned Albert Verheyden coldly, as he retired towards a window, somewhat repelled by the too freely proffered acquaintance of the Skipper, and the rather loud voice and obtrusive manner with which he addressed those around him.

"Oh, this craft of singing is the touchstone of gentility now-a-days," said Cocklescraft, twirling his velvet bonnet by the gold tassel appended to the crown. "A man is accounted unfurnished who has no skill in that joyous art. Sea-bred as I am, Collector—worshipful Master Warden—you would scarce believe me, but I have touched lute and guitar myself, and passably well. I learned this trick in Milan, whither I have twice gone in my voyages, and dwelt there with these Italians, some good summer months. That is your climate for dark eyes and bright nights—balconies, and damsels behind the lattice, listening to thrummers and singers upon the pavements below. And upon occasion, we wear the short cloak and dagger. I have worn cloak and stiletto in my travels, Master Collector, and trolled a catch in the true tongue of Tuscany, when tuck and rapier rung in the burden. The hot blood there is a commodity which the breeze from the Alps hath no virtue to cool, as it doth in Switzerland."

"We will try your singing craft ere it be long," replied the Collector. "We will put you to catch and glee, with a jig to the heel of it, Richard Cocklescraft. You must know, Blanche is eighteen on the festival of St. Therese, and we have a junketing forward which has set the whole province astir. You shall take part in the sport with the town's-people, Master Skipper; and I warrant you find no rest of limb until you show us some new antics of the fashion which you have picked up abroad. You shall dance and sing with witnesses—or a good leg and a topping voice shall have no virtue! I pray you do not forget to make one of our company on the festival of St. Therese. Your gewgaws, Richard, and woman's gear, could not be more in season: every wench in the port is like to be your debtor."

"Thanks, Master Collector, I have a foot and voice, ay, and hand, ever at the service of your good company. I will be first to come and last to depart.—I have been mindful of the Rose of St. Mary's in my voyaging," he said in a respectful and lowered tone, as he approached the maiden. "Mistress Blanche is never so far out of my thoughts that I might come back to the Port without some token for her. I would crave your acceptance of a pretty mantle of crimson silk lined with minever. I found it in Dort, and being taken with its beauty, and thinking how well it would become the gay figure of my pretty mistress of the Rose Croft, I brought it away, and now make bold to ask—that is, if it be agreeable to Mistress Blanche, and if I do not venture too far—that I may be allowed to bring it hither."

"You may find a worthier hand for such a favour," said Blanche, with a tone and look that somewhat eagerly repelled the proffered gift, and manifested dislike of the liberty which the Skipper had taken—a liberty which was in no degree lessened to her apprehension by the unaccustomed gentleness of his voice, and the humble and faltering manner in which he had asked her consent to the present. "I am unused to such gaudy trappings, and should not be content to wear the cloak;" then perceiving some reproof, as she fancied, in the countenance of her sister Alice and the Lady Maria, she added, in a kindlier voice, "I dare not accept it at your hand, Master Skipper."

"Nay," replied Cocklescraft, presuming upon the mildness of the maiden's last speech, and pressing the matter with that obtrusiveness which marked his character and nurture, "I shall not take it kindly if thou dost not;" and as a flush overspread his cheek, he added, "I counted to a certainty that you would do me this courtesy."

"Men sometimes count rashly, Master Cocklescraft," interposed the Lady Maria, "who presume upon a maiden's willingness to incur such debts."

"Save you, madam," replied the Skipper; "I should be sorry Mistress Blanche should deem it to be incurring a debt."

"I have not been trained," said Blanche, with perfect self-possession and firmness of manner, which she intended should put an end to the Skipper's importunity, "to receive such favours from the hand of a stranger; when I have need of a mantle, the mercer shall be my friend."

"You will, perchance, think better of it when you see the mantle," said the Skipper, carelessly, and then added with a saucy smile, "women are changeful, Master Collector; I will bring the gewgaw for Mistress Blanche's inspection—a chapman may have that privilege."

"You may spare yourself the trouble," said the maiden.

"Nay, mistress, think it not a trouble, I beseech you; I count nothing a trouble which shall allow me to please thy fancy." As the Skipper uttered this he came still nearer to the chair on which Blanche was seated, and, almost in a whisper, said, "I pray you, mistress, think not so lightly of my wish to serve you. I have set my heart upon your taking the mantle."

"Master Skipper, a word with you," interrupted the Secretary, who had watched the whole scene; and aware of the annoyance which Cocklescraft's rudeness inflicted upon the maiden, had quietly approached him and now beckoned him to a recess of the window, where they might converse without being heard by the company. "It is not civil to importune the lady in this fashion. You must be satisfied with her answer as she has given it to you. It vexes the daughter of Master Warden to be thus besought. I pray you, sir, no more of it."

Cocklescraft eyed the Secretary for a moment with a glance of scornful resentment, and then replied in a voice inaudible to all but the person to whom it was addressed. "Right! perhaps you are right, sir; but when I would be tutored for my behaviour, he shall be a man, by my troth, who takes that duty on him, and shall wear a beard and sword both. I needed not thy schooling, master crotchet-monger!" Then leaving the Secretary, he strode towards the maiden, and assuming a laughing face, which but awkwardly concealed his vexation, he said, "well, Mistress Blanche, since you are resolved that you will not take my poor bauble off my hands, I must give it over as a venture lost, and so an end of it. I were a fool to be vexed because I could not read the riddle of a maiden's fancy: how should such fish of the sea be learned in so gentle a study? So, viaggio, it shall break no leg of mine! I will dance none the less merrily for it at the feast: and as for the mantle, why it may find other shoulders in the Port, though it shall never find them so fit to wear it withal, as the pretty shoulders of Mistress Blanche. Master Warden I must fain take my leave; my people wait me at the quay. Fair weather for the feast, and a merry time of it, ladies! A Dios, Master Collector!"

The gaiety of this leaving-taking was dashed with a sternness of manner which all the Skipper's acting could not conceal, and as he walked towards the door, he paused a moment to touch Albert Verheyden's cloak and whispered in his ear, "We shall be better acquainted, sir;" then leaving the house he rapidly shaped his course towards the town.

He had scarcely got out of sight before Blanche sprang from her chair and ran towards her father, pouring out upon him a volley of reproof for his unadvised and especially unauthorized invitation of the Skipper to the festival. The maiden was joined in this assault by her auxiliaries, the Proprietary's sister and Mistress Alice, who concurred in reading the simple-minded and unconsciously offending old gentleman a lecture upon his improvident interference in this delicate matter. They insisted that Cocklescraft's associations in the port gave him no claim to such a favour, and that, at all events, it was Blanche's prerogative to be consulted in regard to the admission of the younger and gayer portions of her company.

"Have you not had your will, my dear father," was the summing up of Blanche's playful attack, "to your full content, in summoning all the old humdrum folks of the province, even to the Dominie and his wife, who have never been known to go to a merry-making any where, and who are both so deaf that they have not heard each other speak this many a day? and now you must needs be bringing the Skipper hither."

"Lackaday, wench! what have I done to redden thy brow?" interrupted Mr. Warden, with a face of perplexed good humour, unable longer to bear the storm of rebuke, or to parry the arguments which were so eagerly thrust at him; "I warrant now I have made mischief without knowing how! The Skipper is a free blade, of good metal, and of a figure, too, which, methinks, might please a damsel in a dance, and spare us all this coil; his leg has not its fellow in the province. You take me to task roundly, when all the while I was so foolish as to believe I was doing you regardful service."

"He hath a wicked look, father," was Blanche's reply; "and a saucy freedom which I like not. He is ever too bold in his greeting, and lacks gentle breeding. He must come to me, forsooth, with his mantle, as an especial token, and set upon me with so much constancy to take it! Take a mantle from him! I have never even seen him but twice before, and then it was in church, where he must needs claim to speak to me as if he were an old acquaintance! I will none of him nor his mantle, if he were fifty times a properer man than he is!"

"Be it so, my daughter," replied the Collector. "But we must bear this mishap cheerily. I will not offend again. You women," he said, as he walked to and fro through the parlour, with his hands behind his back, and a good natured smile playing over his features, "you women are more shrewd to read the qualities of men, especially in matters touching behaviour, than such old pock-puddings as I am. I will be better counselled before I trespass in this sort again. But remember, Blanche, the Skipper has his summons, and our hospitality must not suffer reproach; so we will e'en make the best we can of this blundering misadventure of mine. For our own honour, we must be courteous, Blanche, to the Skipper; and, therefore, do thou take heed that he have no cause to say we slight him. As I get old I shall grow wise."

Blanche threw her arms around her father's neck and imprinting a kiss upon his brow, said in a tone of affectionate playfulness, "for your sake, dear father, I will not chide: the Skipper shall not want due observance from me. I did but speak to give you a caution, by which you shall learn that the maidens of this province are so foolish as to stand to it, and I amongst the rest, that they are better able to choose their gallants than their fathers,—though their fathers be amongst his Lordship's most trusty advisers."

"Now a thousand benisons upon thy head, my child!" said the Collector, as he laid his hand upon Blanche's glossy locks, and then left the apartment.

CHAPTER XV

Friend to the sea, and foeman sworn
To all that on her waves are borne,
When falls a mate in battle broil
His comrade heirs his portioned spoil—
Chalice and plate from churches borne,
And gems from shrieking beauty torn,
Each string of pearl, each silver bar,
And all the wealth of western war.

Rokeby.

As the Skipper strode towards the town, his dogged air and lowering brow evinced the disquiet of his spirit at what had just occurred. He was nettled by the maiden's rejection of his proffered gift, and a still deeper feeling of resentment agitated his mind against the Secretary. Far other man was he than he was deemed by the burghers of St. Mary's. In truth, they knew but little more of him than might be gained from his few occasional visits to the port in a calling which, as it brought him a fair harvest of profit, laid him under a necessity to cultivate, for the nonce, the good opinion of his customers by such address as he was master of.

Cocklescraft belonged to that tribe of desperate men, until near this period in the full career of their bloody successes, known as "The Brethren of the Coast." His first breath was drawn upon the billows of the ocean, and his infancy was nursed in the haunts of the buccaneers, amongst the Keys of the Bahamas. When but a lad, attending upon these wild hordes in their expeditions against the commerce of the Gulf, he chanced to attract the notice of the famous Captain Morgan, whilst that most rapacious of all the pirate leaders was preparing, at Jamaica, for his incursion against Maracaibo. The freebooter was charmed with the precocious relish for rapine conspicuous in the character of the boy; and, with an affectionate interest, took him under his tutelage, assigning to him a post near his person, rather of pageantry than service—that of a page or armour-bearer, according to the yet lingering forms of chivalry. The incredible bravery of the buccaneers in this exploit, and their detestable cruelties were witnessed by this callow imp of the sea, with a delight and a shrewdness of apprehension which gave to his youthful nature the full benefit of the lesson. He was scarce two years older when, in the due succession of his hopeful experience, he again attended his patron upon that unmatched adventure of plunder and outrage, the leaguer of Panama; and it was remarked that amidst the perils of the cruise upon the Costa Rica, the toils of the inland march over moor and mountain, and the desperate hazards of the storming of the city, the page, graceful and active as the minion of a lady's bower, and fierce as a young sea-wolf, was seen every where, like an elvish sprite, tracking the footsteps of his ruthless master. The history of human wickedness has not a more appalling chapter than that which records the fate of the wretched inhabitants of Panama in this assault; and yet, in the midst of its shocking enormities, the gay and tasseled familiar of the ruffian pirate chief tripped daintily through the carnage, with the light step of a reveller, and pursued the flying virgins and affrighted matrons, from house to house, as the flames enveloped their roof trees, with the mockery and prankishness of an actor in a masquerade. This expedition terminated not without adding another item to the experience of the young free-booter—the only one, perhaps, yet wanting to his perfect accomplishment. The Welsh Captain, laden with spoils of untold value, played false to his comrades, by stealing off with the lion's share of the booty; thus, by a gainful act of perfidy, inculcating upon the eager susceptibility of the page an imposing moral, of which it may be supposed he would not be slow to profit.

Such was the school in which Cocklescraft received the rudiments of his education. These harsher traits of his character, however, it is but justice to say, were, in some degree, mitigated by a tolerably fair amount of scholastic accomplishment, picked up in the intervals of his busy life amongst the scant teaching afforded by the islands, of which the protection and care of his patron enabled him to profit. To this was added no mean skill in music, dancing, and the use of his weapon; whilst a certain enthusiasm of temperament stimulated his courage and even whetted the fierceness of his nature.

Morgan, having run his career, returned to England, a man of wealth, and was knighted by the monarch, in one of those profligate revels by which Charles disgraced his kingly state; the page was, in consequence, turned adrift upon the world, as it is usual to say of heroes, "with no fortune but his talents, and no friend but his sword." Riot soon exhausted his stock of plunder, and the prodigal licentiousness of "The Brethren of the Coast," forbade the gathering of a future hoard. About this date the European powers began to deal more resolutely with the banditti of the islands, and their trade consequently became more precarious. They were compelled, in pursuit of new fields for robbery, to cross the isthmus and try their fortunes on the coast of the Pacific—whither Cocklescraft followed and reaped his harvest in the ravage of Peru: but in turn, the Brethren found themselves tracked into these remoter seas, and our adventurer was fain, with many of his comrades, to find his way back to the coves and secret harbours of Tortuga and the Keys, whence he contrived to eke out a scant subsistence, by an occasional stoop upon such defenceless wanderers of the ocean as chance threw within his grasp. The Olive Branch was a beautiful light vessel, which, in one of his sea-forays, he had wrested from a luckless merchant; and this acquisition suggested to him the thought that, with such necessary alterations as should disguise her figure and equipment, he might drive a more secure, and, perchance, more profitable trade between the Atlantic colonies and the old countries; so, with a mongrel crew of trusty cutthroats, carefully selected from the companions of his former fortunes, and a secret armament well bestowed for sudden emergency, he set himself up for an occasional trader between the Chesapeake and the coast of Holland. A lucky acquaintance with the Cripple of St. Jerome's gave him a useful ally in his vocation as a smuggler; the fisherman's hut, long believed to be the haunt of evil spirits, admirably favoured his design, and under the management of Rob, soon became a spot of peculiar desecration in popular report; and thus, in no long space of time, the gay, swashing cavalier, master of the Olive Branch, began to find good account in his change of character from the Flibustier of the Keys into that of smuggler and trader of the Chesapeake. He had now made several voyages from St. Mary's to the various marts of Holland and England, taking out cargoes of tobacco and bringing back such merchandise as was likely to find a ready sale in the colonies. His absence from port was often mysteriously prolonged, and on his return it not unfrequently happened that there were found amongst his cargo commodities such as might scarce be conjectured to have been brought from the ports of Europe,—consisting some times of tropical fruits, ingots of gold and silver, and sundry rich furniture of Indian aspect, better fitted for the cabinet of the virtuoso than the trade of a new province. Then, also, there were occasionally costly stuffs, and tissues of exceeding richness, such as cloth of gold, velvets of Genoa, arras tapestry, and even pictures which might have hung in churches. These commodities were invariably landed at St. Jerome's Bay before the Olive Branch cast her anchor in the harbour of St. Mary's, and were reshipped on the outward voyage. The Cripple of St. Jerome's had a few customers who were privileged at certain periods to traffic with him in a species of merchandise of which he was seldom without a supply at his command—chiefly wines and strong waters, and coarser household goods, which were charily exhibited in small parcels at the hut, and when the bargain was made, supplied in greater bulk by unseen hands from secret magazines, concerning which the customer was not so rash as even to inquire—for Rob was a man who, the country people most devoutly believed, had immediate commerce with the Evil One, and who, it was known, would use his dagger before he gave warning by words.

The open and lawful dealing of the Skipper, in the port of St. Mary's, had brought him into an acquaintance with most of the inhabitants, and as his arrival was always a subject of agreeable expectation, he was, by a natural consequence, looked upon with a friendly regard. His address, gaiety of demeanour, and fine figure—which last was studiously set off to great advantage by a rich and graceful costume—heightened this sentiment of personal favour, and gave him privileges in the society of the town which, in that age of scrupulous regard to rank, would have been denied him if he had been a constant sojourner. Emboldened by this reception he had essayed to offer some gallant civilities to the maiden of the Rose Croft, which were instantly repelled, however, by the most formal coldness. The Skipper was not so practised an observer as to perceive in this repugnance, the actual aversion which the maiden felt against his advances to acquaintance; and he was content to account it a merely girlish reserve which importunity and assiduous devotion might overcome. His vanity suggested the resolve to conquer the damsel's indifference; and as that thought grew upon his fancy, it, by degrees, ripened into a settled purpose, which in the end completely engrossed his mind. As he brooded over the subject, and permitted his imagination to linger around that form of beauty and loveliness,—cherished as it was, during the long weeks of his lonely tracking of the sea, and in the solitary musings and silent night-watches of his deck,—a romantic ardour was kindled in his breast, and he hastened back to the Port of St. Mary's, strangely wrought upon by new impulses, which seemed to have humanized and mellowed even his rude nature: the shrewder observers were aware of more gentleness in his bearing, though they found him more wayward in his temper;—he was prouder of heart, yet with humbler speech, and often more stern than before. The awakening of a new passion had overmastered both the ferocity and the levity of his character. He was, in truth, the undivulged, anxious, and almost worshipping lover of Blanche Warden.

When such a nature as I have described chances to fall into the loving vein, it will be admitted to be a somewhat fearful category both for the lady and the lover's rival. Such men are not apt to mince matters in the course of their wooing.

This was the person who now plied his way towards the port, in solitary rumination over two distinct topics of private grief, each of a nature to rouse the angry devil of his bosom. He could not but see that his first approach towards the favour of his mistress had been promptly repelled. That alone would have filled his mind with bitterness, and given a harsh complexion to his thoughts;—but this cause of complaint was almost stifled by the more engrossing sentiment of hostility against the Secretary. That he should have been rebuked for his behaviour, by a man,—and a man, too, who evidently stood well with the lady of his love; taken to task and chid in the very presence of his mistress,—was an offence that called immediately to his manhood and demanded redress. Such redress was more to his hand than the nicer subtleties of weighing the maiden's displeasure, and he turned to it with a natural alacrity, as to a comfort in his perplexity. It is the instinct of a rude nature to refer all cases of wounded sensibility to the relief of battle. A rejected lover, like a child who has lost a toy, finds consolation in his distress by fighting any one that he can persuade himself has stood in his way, and he is made happy when there chances to be some plausible ground for such a proceeding. The Skipper thought the subject over in every aspect which his offended pride could fancy. At one moment the idea of quarrel with the Secretary pleased him, and almost reconciled him to the maiden's coldness; at the next he doubted whether, after all, she had in fact designed to repel his friendship. He vibrated between these considerations for a space in silence: his pride quelled the expression of his anger. But by degrees his quickened pace and sturdier step, and, now and then, that slight shake of the head by which men sometimes express determination, made it plain that the fiery element in his bosom was rising in tumult. At length, unable to suppress his feeling, the inward commotion found utterance in words.

"Who and what is this Master Secretary that hath set the maiden of the Rose Croft to look upon me with an evil spirit? I would fain know if he think himself a properer man than I. Doth he stand upon his fingering of a lute, and his skill to dance?—Why even in this chamber-craft I will put it to a wager he is no master of mine. Is he more personable in shape or figure?—goes he in better apparel? or is that broken English of his more natural to the province than my plain speech, that he should claim the right to chide me for my behaviour? Is it that he hath a place in the train of his Lordship? Have not I served as near to a belted knight—lord of a thousand stout hearts and master of a fleet of thirty sail?—ay, and in straits where you should as soon expect to meet a hare as that crotchet-monger. A bookish clerk with no manly calling that should soil his ruff in the space of a moon! By Saint Iago, but I will put him to his books to learn how he shall heal the stroke of a choleric hand, when the time shall serve to give him the taste of it!—Mistress Blanche would not be importuned—indeed! And he must be my tutor to teach me what pleaseth Mistress Blanche. He lied—the maiden did not mislike my question;—she but hung her head to have it so openly spoken. I know she doth not set at naught my favours, but as damsels from custom do a too public tender of a token. Old Anthony Warden counts his friends by their manhood, and he hath shown me grace:—his daughter in the end will follow his likings—and as the father's choice approves, so will hers incline. Am I less worthy in old Master Warden's eyes, than yonder parchment bearer—that pen-and-ink slave of his Lordship's occasions?—he that durst not raise his eye above his Lord's shoe, nor speak out of a whisper when his betters are in presence? What is he, to put me from the following of my own will when it pleases me to speak to any maiden of this province?—I am of the sea—the broad, deep sea! she hath nursed me in her bosom,—and hath given me my birth-right to be as proudly borne as the honours of any lord of the land. I have a brave deck for my foot, a good blade for my belt, the bountiful ocean before me and a score of merry men at my back. Are these conditions so mean that I must brook the Secretary's displeasure or fashion my speech to suit his liking?—We shall understand each other better, in good time, or I shall lack opportunity to speak my mind:—I shall, good Master Verheyden,—you have the word of a 'Brother of the Bloody Coast' for that!"

Before the Skipper had ceased this petulant and resentful self-communion, he found himself in the neighbourhood of the Catholic Chapel, nearly in front of the dwelling of father Pierre, when the good priest, who was at this moment returning from noon-day service, took him at unawares with the salutation,—

"Peace be with you, son!—you reckon up the sum of your ventures with a careful brow, and speak loud enough to make the town acquainted with thy gains, if perchance some of the chapmen with whom thou hast dealing should be in thy path. How fares it with thee, Master Skipper?"

"Ha, Mi Padre!" exclaimed Cocklescraft, instantly throwing aside his graver thoughts and assuming a jocular tone. "Well met;—I was on my way to visit you: that would I have done yesterday upon my arrival, but that the press of my business would not allow it. You grow old, father, so evenly that, although I see you but after long partings, I can count no fresh touch of time upon your head."

"Men of your calling should not flatter," said the priest smiling. "What news do you bring us from the old world?"

"Oh, much and merry, father Pierre. The old world plies her old trade and thrives by it. Knavery hath got somewhat of the upper hand since they have quit crossing swords in this new piece of Nimeguen. The Hogan Mogans are looking a little surly at the Frenchman for cocking his beaver so bravely; and our jobbernowl English, now that they can find no more reason to throttle each other, have gone back to their old sport of pricking the side of our poor church. You shall find as many plots in London, made out of hand and ready for use in one month, as would serve all the stage plays of the kingdom for the next hundred years—and every plot shall have a vile Papist at the bottom of it,—if you may believe Oates and Bedloe. I was there when my Lord Stafford was made a head shorter on Tower Hill. You heard of this,—father?"

"Alack! in sorrow we heard of this violence," replied the priest, "and deeply did it grieve my Lord to lose so good a friend. Even as you have found it in England, so is it here. The discontents against the holy church are nursed by many who seek thereby to command the province. We have plotters here who do not scruple to contrive against the life of his Lordship and his Lordship's brother the Chancellor. Besides, the government at home is unfriendly to us."

"You have late news from England?" inquired the Skipper.

"We have,—and which, but that you are true in your creed, I might scarce mention to your ear—the royal order has come to my Lord to dismiss his Catholic servants from office—every one. His Lordship scruples to obey. This, Master Skipper, I confide to you in private, as not to be told again."

"To remove all!" said Cocklescraft. "Why it will sweep off his nearest friends—Anthony Warden and all."

"Even so."

"There is fighting matter in that, upon the spot," exclaimed the Skipper. "By St. Sebastian, I hope it may come up while I am in port! The Collector, old as he is, will buckle on his toledo in that quarrel. He has mettle for it; and I could wish no better play than to stand by his side. Who is this Secretary of my Lord's private chamber? I met him at the Collector's to-day."

"Master Albert Verheyden," replied the priest.

"I know his name—they told it to me there—but his quality and condition, father?"

"You may be proud of his fellowship," said father Pierre; "he was once a scholar of the Jesuit school at Antwerp, of the class inscribed 'Princeps Diligentiæ,' and brought thence by my Lord. A youth, Master Cocklescraft, of promise and discretion—a model to such as would learn good manners and cherish virtuous inclinations. You may scarcely fail to see him at the Collector's: the townspeople do say he has an eye somewhat dazzled there."

"Craving pardon for my freedom, I say, father Pierre, a fig's end for such a model!" exclaimed the Skipper, pettishly: "you may have such by the score, wherever lazy, bookish men eat their bread. I like him not, with his laced band and feather, his book and lute: harquebuss and whinyard are the tools for these days. I hear the Fendalls have been at mischief again. We shall come to bilbo and buff before long. Your Secretary will do marvellous service in these straits, father."

"Son, you are somewhat sinful in your scorn," said the priest, mildly; "the Secretary doth not deserve this taunt——"

"By the holy hermits, father, I speak of the Secretary but as I think. He does not awe me with his greatness. I vail no topsail to him, I give you my word for it."

"The saints preserve us from harm!" said the churchman. "We know not what may befall us from the might of our enemies, when this hot blood shall sunder our friends. In sober counsel, son, and not in rash divisions shall we find our safety. It doth not become thee, Master Cocklescraft, to let thy tetchy humour rouse thee against the Secretary. It might warrant my displeasure."

"Mea culpa, holy father—I do confess my fault," said the seaman, in a tone of assumed self-constraint—"I will not again offend; and for my present atonement will offer a censer of pure silver, which in my travels I picked up, and in truth did then design to give, to the Chapel of St. Mary's. I will bring it to the chapel, father Pierre, as soon as my vessel is unladen."

"You should offer up your anger too, to make this gift acceptable," returned the priest. "Let thy dedication be with a cleansed heart."

"Ha, father Pierre," said the Skipper, jocularly; "my conscience does easily cast off a burden: so it shall be as you command. I did not tell you that whilst my brigantine lay in the Helder, I made a land flight to Louvaine, where a certain Abbot of Andoyne,—a pious, somewhat aged, and, thanks to a wholesome refectory! a good jolly priest,—hearing I came from the province, must needs send for me to ask if I knew father Pierre de la Maise, and upon my answer, that I did right well, he begs me to bring his remembrance back to you."

"I knew father Gervase," replied the priest with a countenance full of benignity—"some forty years ago, when he was a reader in the Chair of St. Isidore at Rome. He remembers me?—a blessing on his head!—and he wears well, Master Skipper?"

"Quite as well as yourself," replied Cocklescraft. "Father, a cup of your cool water, and I will depart," he said, as he helped himself to the draught. "I will take heed to what you have said touching the royal order—and by St. Iago, I will be a friend in need to the Collector. Master Verheyden shall not be a better one. Now fare thee well, father. Peregrine Cadger shall have order to cut you off a cassock from the best cloth I have brought him, and little Abbot the tailor shall put it in fashion for you."

"You are lavish of your bounties, son," replied the priest, taking Cocklescraft by both hands as he was now about to withdraw. "You have a poor churchman's thanks. It gives me comfort to be so considered, and I prize your kindness more than the cassock. A blessing on thy ways, Master Cocklescraft!"

The Skipper once more set forth on his way towards the port; and with a temper somewhat allayed by the acting of the scene I have just described, though with no abatement of the resentment which rankled at the bottom of his heart, even under the smiling face and gay outside which he could assume with the skill of a consummate dissembler, he soon reached the Crow and Archer. From thence he meditated, as soon as his occasions would permit, a visit to the Cripple of St. Jerome's.

CHAPTER XVI

"Who be these, sir?"
"Fellows to mount a bank. Did your instructer
In the dear tongues never discourse to you
Of the Italian mountebanks?"
"Yes, sir."
"Why here you shall see one."
"They are quacksalvers,
Fellows that live by venting oils and drugs."
Volpone.

The council had been summoned to meet on the morning following that of the incidents related in the last chapter, and the members were now accordingly assembling, soon after breakfast, at the Proprietary mansion. The arrival of one or two gentlemen on horseback with their servants, added somewhat to the bustle of the stable yard, which was already the scene of that kind of busy idleness and lounging occupation so agreeable to the menials of a large establishment. Here, in one quarter, a few noisy grooms were collected around the watering troughs, administering the discipline of the curry-comb or the wash bucket to some half score of horses. In a corner of the yard Dick Pagan the courier and Willy o' the Flats, with the zeal of amateur vagrants, were striving to cozen each other out of their coppers at the old game of Cross and Pile; whilst, in an opposite direction, Derrick was exhibiting to a group of spectators, amongst whom the young heir apparent was a prominent personage, a new set of hawk bells just brought by the Olive Branch from Dort, and lecturing, with a learned gravity, upon their qualities, to the infinite edification and delight of his youthful pupil. Slouching fox hounds, thick-lipped mastiffs and wire-haired terriers mingled indiscriminately amongst these groups, as if confident of that favouritism which is the universal privilege of the canine race amongst good tempered persons and contented idlers all the world over. Whilst the inhabitants of the yard were engrossed with these occupations, a trumpet was heard at a distance in the direction of the town. The blast came so feebly upon the ear as, at first, to pass unregarded, but being repeated at short intervals, and at every repetition growing louder, it soon arrested the general attention, and caused an inquiry from all quarters into the meaning of so unusual an incident.

"Fore God, I think that there be an alarm of Indians in the town!" exclaimed the falconer as he spread his hand behind his ear and listened for some moments, with a solemn and portentous visage. "Look to it, lads—there may be harm afoot. Put up thy halfpence, Dick Pagan, and run forward to seek out the cause of this trumpeting. I will wager it means mischief, masters."

"Indians!" said Willy; "Derrick's five wits have gone on a fool's errand ever since the murder of that family at the Zachaiah fort by the salvages. If the Indians were coming you should hear three guns from Master Randolph Brandt's look-out on the Notley road. It is more likely there may be trouble at the gaol with the townspeople, for there was a whisper afloat yesterday concerning a rescue of the prisoners. Troth, the fellow has a lusty breath who blows that trumpet!"

"Ay, and the trumpet," said Derrick, "is not made to dance with, masters: there is war and throat-cutting in it, or I am no true man."

During this short exchange of conjectures, Dick Pagan had hastened to the gate which opened towards the town, and mounting the post, for the sake of a more extensive view, soon discerned the object of alarm, when, turning towards his companions, he shouted,

"Wounds,—but here's a sight! Pike and musket, belt and saddle, boys! To it quickly;—you shall have rare work anon. Wake up the ban dogs of the fort and get into your harness. Here comes the Dutch Doctor with his trumpeter as fierce as the Dragon of Wantley. Buckle to and stand your ground!"

"Ho, ho!" roared the fiddler with an impudent, swaggering laugh. "Here's a pretty upshot to your valours! Much cry and little wool, like the Devil's hog-shearing at Christmas. You dullards, couldn't I have told you it was the Dutch Doctor,—if your fright had left you but a handful of sense to ask a question? Didn't I see both him and his trumpeter last night at the Crow and Archer, with all their jin-gumbobs in a pair of panniers? Oh, but he is a rare Doctor, and makes such cures, I warrant you, as have never been seen, known or heard of since the days of St. Byno, who built up his own serving man again, sound as a pipkin, after the wild beasts had him for supper."

The trumpet now sent forth a blast which terminated in a long flourish, indicating the approach of the party to the verge within which it might not be allowable to continue such a clamour; and in a few moments afterwards the Doctor with his attendant entered the stable yard. He was a little, sharp-featured, portly man, of a brown, dry complexion, in white periwig, cream-coloured coat, and scarlet small clothes: of a brisk gait, and consequential air, which was heightened by the pompous gesture with which he swayed a gold-mounted cane full as tall as himself. His attendant, a bluff, burly, red-eyed man, with a singularly stolid countenance, tricked out in a grotesque costume, of which a short cloak, steeple-crowned hat and feather, and enormous nether garments, all of striking colours, were the most notable components, bore a brass trumpet suspended on one side, and a box of no inconsiderable dimensions in front of his person; and thus furnished, followed close at the heels of the important individual whose coming had been so authentically announced.

No sooner had the Doctor got fairly within the gate than he was met by Derrick Brown, who, being the most authoritative personage in the yard, took upon himself the office of giving the stranger welcome.

"Frents, how do you do?" was the Doctor's accost in a strong, Low Dutch method of pronouncing English. "I pelieve dis is not de gate I should have entered to see his Lordship de Lord Proprietary," he added, looking about him with some surprise to find where he was.

"If it was my Lord you came to see," said the falconer, "you should have turned to your right, and gone by the road which leads to the front of the house. But the way you have come is no whit the longer: we can take you through, Master Doctor, by the back door."

"Vell, vell, dere is noding lost by peing acquainted at once wid de people of de house," replied the man of medicine; "dere is luck to make your first entrance by de pack door, as de old saying is. I vas summoned dis morning to appear before de council, py my Lord's order; and so, I thought I might trive a little pusiness, at de same time, wid de family."

"I told you all," said Willy, with an air of self-importance at his own penetration, "that this was a rare doctor. The council hath sent for him! my Lord hath made it a state matter to see him. It isn't every doctor that comes before the worshipful council, I trow. Give him welcome, boys, doff your beavers."

At this command several of the domestics touched their hats, with a gesture partly in earnest and partly in sport, as if expecting some diversion to follow.

"No capping to me, my frents!" exclaimed the Doctor, with a bow, greatly pleased at these tokens of respect; "no capping to me! Pusiness is pusiness, and ven I come to sell you tings dat shall do you goot, I tank you for your custom and your money, widout asking you to touch your cap."

"There is sense in that," said John Alward; "and since you come to trade in the yard, Doctor, you can show us your wares. There is a penny to be picked up here."

"Open your box, Doctor; bring out your pennyworths; show us the inside!" demanded several voices at once.

"Ha, ha!" exclaimed the vender of drugs, "you are wise, goot frents; you know somewhat! You would have a peep at my aurum potabiles in dat little casket—my multum in parvo? Yes, you shall see, and you shall hear what you have never seen pefore, and shall not in your long lives again."

"Have you e'er a good cleansing purge for a moulting hawk?" inquired Derrick Brown, whilst the doctor was unlocking the box.

"Or a nostrum that shall be sure work on a horse with a farcy?" asked one of the grooms.

"Hast thou an elixir that shall expel a lumbago?" demanded John Alward: all three speaking at the same instant.

"Tib, the cook," said a fourth, "has been so sore beset with cramps, that only this morning she was saying, in her heart she believed she would not stop to give the paste buckle that Tom Oxcart gave her for a token at Whitsuntide, for a cordial that would touch a cold stomach. I will persuade her into a trade with the Doctor."

"Oh, as for the women," replied a fifth, "there isn't a wench in my Lord's service that hasn't a bad tooth, or a cold stomach, or a tingling in the ears, or some such ailing: it is their nature—they would swallow the Doctor's pack in a week, if they had license."

The man of nostrums was too much employed in opening out his commodities to heed the volley of questions which were poured upon him all round, but having now put himself in position for action, he addressed himself to his auditors:

"I vill answer all your questions in goot time; but I must crave your leave, frents, to pegin in de order of my pusiness. Dobel," he said, turning to his attendant, who stood some paces in the rear, "come forward and pegin."

The adjutant at this command stepped into the middle of the ring, and after making several strange grimaces, of which at first view his countenance would have been deemed altogether incapable, and bowing in three distinct quarters to the company, commenced the following speech:

"Goot beoplish!"—this was accompanied with a comic leer that set the whole yard in a roar—"dish ish de drice renowned und ingomprbl Doctor Closh Tebor"—another grimace, and another volley of laughter—"what ish de grand pheseeshan of de greate gofernor of New York, Antony Prockolls, und lives in Alpany in de gofernor's own pallash, wid doo tousand guilders allowed him py de gofernor everich yeere, und a goach to rite, und a pody-cart to go pefore him in de sthreets ven he valks to take de air. All tish to keepe de gofernor und his vrouw de Laty Katerina Prockholls in goot healf—noding else—on mein onor." This was said with great emphasis, the speaker laying his hand on his heart and making a bow, accompanied with a still more ludicrous grimace than any he had yet exhibited, which brought forth a still louder peal from his auditory.

He was about to proceed with his commendatory harangue, when he was interrupted by Benedict Leonard. It seems that upon the first announcement by the Doctor of the purport of his visit, the youth, fearful lest his mother, who was constitutionally subject to alarm, might have been disturbed by the trumpet, ran off to apprise her of what he had just witnessed; and giving her the full advantage of Willy's exaggerated estimate of the travelling healer of disease, returned, by the lady's command, to conduct this worthy into her presence. He accordingly now delivered his message, and forthwith master and man moved towards the mansion, with the whole troop of the stable yard at their heels.

The itinerant was introduced into Lady Baltimore's presence in a small parlour, where she was attended by two little girls, her only children beside the boy we have noticed, and the sister of the Proprietary. Her pale and emaciated frame and care-worn visage disclosed to the practised glance of the visiter a facile subject for his delusive art,—a ready votary of that credulous experimentalism which has filled the world with victims to medical imposture. In the professor of medicine's reverence to the persons before him there was an overstrained obsequiousness, but, at the same time, an expression of imperturbable confidence fully according with the ostentatious pretension which marked his demeanour amongst the menials of the household. Notwithstanding his broad accent, he spoke with a ready fluency that showed him well skilled in that voluble art by which, at that day, the workers of wonderful cures and the possessors of infallible elixirs advertised the astonishing virtues of their compounds—an art which has in our time only changed its manner of utterance, and now announces its ridiculous pretensions in every newspaper of every part of our land, in whole columns of mountebank lies and quack puffery.

"This is the great Doctor," said Benedict Leonard, who now acted as gentleman usher, "and he has come I can't tell how far, to see who was ailing in our parts. I just whispered to him, dear mother, what a famous good friend you were to all sorts of new cures. And oh, it would do you good to see what a box of crankums he has in the hall! Yes, and a man to carry it, with a trumpet! Blowing and physicking a plenty now, to them that like it! How the man bears such a load, I can't guess."

"Dobel has a strong back and a steady mule for his occasions, my pretty poy," said the Doctor, patting the heir apparent on the head, with a fondness of manner that sensibly flattered the mother. "When we would do goot, master, we must not heed de trouble to seek dem dat stand in need of our ministrations over de world."

The lady's feeble countenance lit up with a sickly smile as she remonstrated with the boy. "Bridle thy tongue, Benedict, nor suffer it to run so nimbly. We have heard, Doctor, something of your fame, and gladly give you welcome."

"Noble lady," replied the pharmacopolist, "I am but a simple and poor Doctor, wid such little fame as it has pleased Got to pestow for mine enteavours to miticate de distemperatures and maladies and infirmities which de fall of man, in de days of Adam, de august progenitor of de human races, has prought upon all his children. And de great happiness I have had to make many most wonderful cures in de provinces of America, made me more pold to hope I might pring some assuagement and relief to your ladyship, who, I have peen told, has peen grievously tormented wid perturbations and melancholics; a very common affection wid honourable ladies."

"Alack, Doctor, my affections come from causes which are beyond the reach of your art," said the lady with a sigh. "Still, it would please me to hear the cures you speak of. You have, doubtless, had great experience?"

"You shall hear, my lady. I am not one of dat rabble of pretenders what travel apout de world to cry up and magnify dere own praises. De Hemel is mij getuige,—Heaven is my chudge, and your ladyship's far renowned excellent wisdom forbids dat you should be imposed upon by dese cheats and impostors denominated—and most justly, on my wort!—charlatans and empirical scaramouches. De veritable merit in dis world is humble, my lady. I creep rader in de dust, dan soar in de clouts:—it is in my nature. Oders shall speak for me—not myself."

"But you have seen the world, Doctor, and studied, and served in good families?"

"Your ladyship has great penetration. I have always lived in friendship wid worshipful peoples. De honourable Captain General Anthony

Brockholls, de governor of de great province of New York,—hah! dere was nopody could please him but Doctor Debor. Night and day, my lady, for two years, have I peen physicking his excellency and all his family:—de governor is subject to de malady of a pad digestion and crudities which gives him troublesome dreams. I have studied in de school of Leyden—dree courses, until I could find no more to learn; and den I have travelled in France, Germany, and Italy, where I took a seat in de great University of Padua, for de penefit of de lectures of dat very famous doctor, Veslingius, de prefect, your ladyship shall understand, and professor of botany, a most rare herbalist. And dere also I much increased and enriched my learning under de wing of dat astonishing man, de grave and profound Doctor Athelsteinus Leonenas, de expounder of de great secrets of de veins and nerves. You shall chudge, honourable ladies, what was my merit, when I tell you de University would make me Syndicus Artistarum, only dat I refused so great honour, pecause I would not make de envy of my compeers. Did I not say true when I tell you it is not my nature to soar in de clouts?"

"Truly the Doctor hath greatly slighted his fame," said the Lady Maria apart to her kinswoman. "I would fain know what you have in your pack."

"Worshipful madam, you shall soon see," replied the Doctor, who now ordered Dobel, his man, into the room. "Here," he said, as he pointed to the different parcels, "are balsamums, panaceas, and elixirs. Dis is a most noted alexipharmacum against quartan agues, composed of many roots, herps and spices; dis I call de lampas vitæ, an astonishing exhilirator and promoter of de goot humours of de mind, and most valuable for de rare gift of clear sight to de old, wid many oder virtues I will not stop to mention. Dese are confections, electuaries, sirups, conserves, ointments, odoraments, cerates, and gargarisms, for de skin, for de stomach, for de pruises and wounds, for de troat, and every ting pesides. Ah! here, my lady, is de great lapour of my life, de felicity and royal reward—as I may say—of all my studies: it is de most renowned and admired and never-to-be-estimated Medicamentum Promethei, which has done more penefactions dan all de oder simples and compounds in de whole pharmacopeia of medicine. Your ladyship shall take but one half of dis little phial, when you will say more for its praise dan I could speak widout peing accounted a most windy, hyperbolical and monstrous poaster—ha, waarachtig! I will speak noting. Dat wise and sagacious and sapient man, de great governor and captain, Antony Brockholls, has given me in my hand so much as five ducatoons,—yes, my lady, five ducatoons for dat little glass, two hours after a dinner of cold endives—Ik spreek a waarachtiglik—I speak you truly, my lady: and now I give it away for de goot of de world and mine own glory, at no more dan one rix dollar,—five shillings. I do not soar in de clouts?"

"Can you describe its virtues, Doctor?" inquired the lady.

"Mine honoured madam, dey are apundant, and I shall not lie if I say countless and widout number. First, it is a great enemy to plack choler, and to all de affections of de spleen, giving sweet sleep to de eyelids dat have peen kept open py de cares and sufferings and anxieties of de world. It will dispel de charms of witchcraft, magic and sorcery, and turn away de stroke of de evil eye. It corroborates de stomach py driving off de sour humours of de pylorus, and cleansing de diaphram from de oppilations which fill up and torpefy de pipes of de nerves. And your ladyship shall observe dat, as nature has supplied and adapted particular plants and herps to de maladies of de several parts of de animal pody, as,—not to be tedious,—aniseeds and calamint for de head, hysop and liquorice for de lungs, borage for de heart, betony for de spleen, and so on wid de whole pody—dis wonderful medicament contains and possesses in itself someting of all, being de great remedy, antidote and expeller of all diseases, such as vertigine, falling sickness, cramps, catalepsies, lumbagos, rheums, inspissations, agitations, hypocondrics, and tremorcordies, whedder dey come of de head, de heart, de liver, de vena cava, de mesentery or de pericardium, making no difference if dey be hot or cold, dry or moist, or proceeding from terrestrial or genethliacal influences, evil genitures, or vicious aspects of de stars—it is no matter—dey all vanish pefore de great medicamentum. You must know, my lady, dis precious mixture was de great secret—de arcanum mirificabile—of dat wonderful Arabian physician Hamech, which Paracelsus went mad wid cudgelling his prains to find out; and Avicenna and Galen and Trismegistus and Moderatus Columella all proke down in deir search to discover de meaning of de learned worts in which Hamech wrote de signification. De great Swammerdam, hoch! what would he not give Doctor Debor for dat secret! I got it, my lady, from a learned Egyptian doctor, who took it from an eremite of Arabia Felix. It was not my merit, so much as my goot fortune. I am humble, my lady, and do not poast, but speak op't woord van een eerlyk man."

"He discourses beyond our depth," said Lady Baltimore, greatly puzzled to keep pace with the learned pretensions of the quack; "and yet I dare say there is virtue in these medicines. What call you your great compound, Doctor? I have forgotten its name."

"De Medicamentum Promethei," replied the owner of this wonderful treasure, pleased with the interest taken in his discourse. "Your ladyship will comprehend from your reading learned pooks, dat Prometheus was a great headen god, what stole de fire from Heaven, whereby he was able to vivicate and reluminate de decayed and worn-out podies of de human families, and in a manner even to give life to de images of clay; which is all, as your good ladyship discerns, a fabulous narration, or pregnant fable, as de scholars insinuate. And moreover, de poets and philosophers say dat same headen god was very learned in de knowledge of de virtues of plants and herps, which your ladyship will remark is de very consistence and identification of de noble art of pharmacy. Well den, dis Prometheus, my lady—ha, ha!—was some little bit of a juggler, and was very fond of playing his legerdemains wid de gods, till one day de great Jupiter, peing angry wid his jocularities and his tricks, caused him to be chained to a rock, wid a hungry vulture always gnawing his liver; and dere he was in dis great misery, till his pody pined away so small dat his chain would not hold him, and den, aha! he showed Jupiter a goot pair of heels, like an honest fellow, and set apout to find de medicines what should renovate and patch up his liver, which you may be sure he did, my lady, in a very little while. Dis again is anoder fable, to signify dat he was troubled wid a great sickness in dat part of his pody. Now, my lady, see how well de name significates de great virtues of my medicament, which, in de first place, is a miraculous restorer of health and vigour and life to de feeble spirits of de pody: dere's de fire. Second, it is composed of more dan one hundred plants, roots, and seeds, most delicately distilled, sublimed and suffumigated in a limbeck of pure virgin silver, and according to de most subtle projections of alchemy: and dere your ladyship shall see de knowledge of de virtues of plants and de most consummate art of de concoctions. And now for de last significance of de fable: dis medicament is a specific of de highest exaltation for de cure, which never fails, of all distemperatures of de liver; not to say dat it is less potent to overcome and destroy all de oder diseases I have mentioned, and many more. Dere you see de whole Medicamentum Promethei, which I sell to worshipful peoples for one rix dollar de phial. Is it not well named, my lady, and superlative cheap? I give it away: de projection alone costs me more dan I ask for de compound."

"The name is curiously made out," said the lady, "and worthily, if the virtue of the compound answer the description. But your cures, you have not yet touched upon them. I long to hear what notable feats you have accomplished in that sort."

"My man Dobel shall speak," replied the professor. "De great Heaven forpid I should pe a poaster to de ears of such honourable ladies! Dobel, rehearse de great penefaction of de medicament upon de excellent and discreet and virtuous vrouw of Governor Brockholls—Spreek op eene verstaanbare wijze!"

"Hier ben ik," answered Dobel to this summons, stepping at the same time into the middle of the room and erecting his person as stiffly as a grenadier on parade: "Goot beoplish! dish ish de drice renowned und ingomprbl Doctor Closh Tebor— —"

"Stop, stop, hou stil! halt—volslagen gek!" exclaimed the Doctor, horrified at the nature of the harangue his stupid servitor had commenced, and which for a moment threatened to continue, in spite of the violent remonstrance of the master, Dobel persevering like a thing spoken from rather than a thing that speaks—"Fool, jack-pudding! you pelieve yourself on a bank, up on a stage, before de rabble rout? You would disgrace me before honourable and noble ladies, wid your tavern howlings, and your parkings and your pellowings! Out of de door, pegone!"

The imperturbable and stolid trumpeter, having thus unfortunately incurred his patron's ire, slunk from the parlour, utterly at a loss to comprehend wherein he had offended. The Doctor in the mean while, overwhelmed with confusion and mortified vanity, bustled towards the door and there continued to vent imprecations upon the unconscious Dobel, which, as they were uttered in Low Dutch, were altogether incomprehensible to the company, but at the same time were sufficiently ludicrous to produce a hearty laugh from the Lady Maria, and even to excite a partial show of merriment in her companion. Fortunately for the Doctor, in the midst of his embarrassment, a messenger arrived to inform him that his presence was required before the council, in another part of the house, which order, although it deprived the ladies of the present opportunity of learning the great efficacy of the Medicamentum Promethei in the case of the wife of Governor Brockholls, gave the Doctor a chance of recovering his self-possession by a retreat from the apartment. So, after an earnest entreaty to be forgiven for the inexpert address of his man, and a promise to resume his discourse on a future occasion, he betook himself, under the guidance of the messenger, to the chamber in which the council were convened.

Here sat the Proprietary, and Philip Calvert, the Chancellor, who were now, with five or six other gentlemen, engaged in the transaction of business of grave import.

Some depredations had been recently committed upon the English by the Indians inhabiting the upper regions of the Susquehanna,—especially by the Sinniquoes, who, in an incursion against the Piscattaways, a friendly tribe in the vicinity of St. Mary's, had advanced into the low country, where they had plundered the dwellings of the settlers and even murdered two or three families. The victims of these outrages happened to be Protestants, and Fendall's party availed themselves of the circumstance, to excite the popular jealousy against Lord Baltimore by circulating the report that these murders were committed by Papists in disguise.

What was therefore but an ordinary though frightful incident of Indian hostility, was thus exaggerated into a crime of deep malignity, peculiarly calculated still more to embitter the party exasperations of the day. This consideration rendered it a subject of eager anxiety, on the part of the Council, to procure the fullest evidence of the hostile designs of the Indians, and thus not only to enable the province to adopt the proper measure for its own safety, but also confute the false report which had imputed to the Catholics so absurd and atrocious a design. A traveller by the name of Launcelot Sakel happened, but two or three days before the present meeting of the Council, to arrive at the port, where he put afloat the story of an intended invasion of the province by certain Indians of New York, belonging to the tribes of the Five Nations, and gave as his authority for this piece of news a Dutch doctor, whom he had fallen in with on the Delaware, where he left him selling nostrums, and who, he affirmed, was in a short space to appear at St. Mary's. This story, with many particulars, was communicated to the Proprietary, which induced the order to summon the Doctor to attend the council as soon after his arrival as possible. In obedience to this summons, our worthy was now in the presence of the high powers of the province, not a little elated with the personal consequence attached to his coming, as well as the very favourable reception he had obtained from the ladies of the household. This consequence was even enhanced by the suite of inquisitive domestics, who followed, at a respectful distance, his movement towards the council chamber, and who, even there, though not venturing to enter, were gathered into a group which from the outside of the door commanded a view of the party within: in the midst of these Willy of the Flats was by no means an unconspicuous personage.

Lord Baltimore received the itinerant physician with that bland and benignant accost which was habitual to him, and proceeded with brief ceremony to interrogate him as to the purport of his visit. The answers were given with a solemn self-complacency, not unmixed with that shrewdness which was an essential attribute to the success of the ancient quacksalver. He described himself as Doctor Claus Debor, a native of Holland, a man of travel, enjoying no mean renown in New York, and, for two years past, a resident of Albany. His chief design in his present journey, he represented to be to disseminate the blessings of his great medicament; whereupon he was about to launch forth into an exuberant tone of panegyric, and had, in fact, already produced a smile at the council board by some high wrought phrases expressive of his incredible labour in the quest of his great secret, when the Proprietary checked his career by a timely admonition.

"Ay, we do not seek to know thy merits as a physician, nor doubt the great virtue of thy drugs, worthy Doctor; but in regard thereto, give thee free permission to make what profit of them you reasonably may in the province. Still, touching this license, I must entreat you, in consideration that my Lady Baltimore has weak nerves, and cannot endure rude noises, to refrain from blowing thy trumpet within hearing of this mansion: besides, our people," he added, looking archly towards the group of domestics, some of whom had now edged into the apartment, "are somewhat faint-hearted at such martial sounds."

"By my troth!" said Willy, in a half whisper to his companions in the entry; "my Lord hath put it to him for want of manners!—I thought as much would come from his tantararas. Listen, you shall hear more anon. Whist!—the Doctor puts on a face—and will have his say, in turn."

"Your very goot and admirable Lordship, mistranslates de significance of my visit," said the Doctor, in his ambitious phrase; "for although I most heartily tank your Lordship's bounty for de permission to sell my inestimable medicament, and which—Got geve het—I do hope shall much advantage my lady wid her weak nerfs and her ailments,—still, I come to opey your most honourable Lordship's summons, which I make pold to pelieve is concerned wid state matters pefore de high and noble council."

"Well, and bravely spoken," said Willy; "and with a good face!—the Doctor holds his own, masters."

"We would hear what you can tell touching a rumour brought to us by one Master Launcelot Sakel, whom you saw at Christina Fort," said the Proprietary.

"There is the point of the matter," whispered Willy, "all in an egg shell."

"Dere is weighty news, my Lord," replied the Doctor. "I have goot reason to pelieve dat de Nordern Indians of New York are meditating and concocting mischief against your Lordship's province."

"Have a care to the truth of your report," said Colonel Talbot, rising from his seat: "it may be worse for you if you be found to trifle with us by passing current a counterfeit story, churned into consistence in your own brain, out of the froth of idle, way-side gossipings. We have a statute against the spreaders of false news."

"Heigh, heigh!—listen to that," said Willy, nudging one of the crowd over whose shoulders he was peering into the room. "There's an outcome with a witness!—there's a flanconade that shall make the Doctor flutter!"

"If I am mendacious," replied the Doctor, "dat is, if I am forgetful of mine respect for trute, dese honourable gentlemens shall teal wid me as a lying pusy pody and pragmatical tale-bearer. Your Lordship shall hear. It is put a fortnight ago, when I was making ready for dis journey, in Alpany, I chanced to see in de town so many as two score, perhaps fifty Indians, who were dere trading skins for powder and shot. Dey reported demselves to be Sinniquoes, and said dey came to talk wid de tribes furder back, to get deir help to fight against de Piscattaways."

"Indeed!—there is probability in that report," said the Proprietary: "well, and how had they sped? what was their success?"

"Some of de Five Nations,—I forget de name of de tribe, my Lord—it might pe de Oneidas—dey told us, promised to march early de next season;—in dere own worts, when de sap pegin to rise."

"In what force, did they say?"

"In large force, my Lord. De Piscattaways, dey said, were frents to my Lord and de English,—and so dey should make clean work wid red and white."

"What more?"

"Dey signified dat dey should have great help from de Delawares and Susquehannocks, who, as I could make it out, wanted to go to war wid your Lordship's peoples at once."

"True; and they have done so. The insolencies of these tribes are already as much as we can endure. Did they find it easy to purchase their powder and lead in Albany? I should hope that traffic would not be allowed."

"My Lord, de traders do not much stop, when dey would turn a penny, to reckon who shall get de loss, so dey get de profit. Dese same Indians I saw afterwards in de town of New York, trading in de same way wid Master Grimes, a merchant."

"Mischief will come of this," said the Proprietary, "unless it be speedily taken in hand. What reason was given by the Northern Indians for joining in this scheme?"

"I tink it was said," replied the Doctor, "dat your Lordship had not made your treaties wid dem, nor sent dem presents, dese two years past."

"True," interposed the Chancellor; "we have failed in that caution—although I have more than once reminded your Lordship of its necessity."

"It shall not be longer delayed," replied the Proprietary. "You are sure, Doctor Debor, these were Sinniquoes you saw?"

"I only know dem by dere own report—I never heard de name pefore. My man Dobel heard dem as well as me; wid your Lordship's permission I shall ask him," said the Doctor, as he went to the door and directed some of the domestics to call the man Dobel.

It happened that Dobel, after his disgrace, had kept apart from the servants of the household, and was now lamenting his misfortune in a voluntary exile on the green at the front door, where Willy of the Flats having hastened to seek him, gave him the order to appear before the council.

"Dobel, you are a made man," he said by way of encouragement; "your master wants you to speak to their honours: and the honourable council want to hear you, Dobel; and so does his Lordship. Hold up thy head, Dobel, and speak for thy manhood—boldly and out, like a buckler man."

"Ya, ya," replied Dobel, whose acquirements in the English tongue were limited to his professional advertisement of Doctor Debor's fame, and a few slender fragments of phrases in common use. Thus admonished by Willy, he proceeded doggedly to the Council Chamber, where as soon as he entered, the Proprietary made a motion to him with his hand to approach the table,—which Dobel interpreting into an order to deliver his sentiments, he forthwith began in a loud voice—

"Goot beoplish! dish is de drice renowned und ingomprbl Doctor——"

Before he had uttered the name, the Doctor's hand was thrust across Dobel's mouth and a volley of Dutch oaths rapped into his ears, at a rate which utterly confounded the poor trumpeter, who was forcibly expelled from the room, almost by a general order. When quiet was restored,—for it may be imagined the scene was not barren of laughter,—the Doctor made a thousand apologies for the stupidity of his servant, and in due time received permission to retire, having delivered all that he was able to say touching the matter in agitation before the Proprietary.

The Council were for some time after this incident engaged in the consideration of the conspiracy against the Proprietary, of which new evidences were every day coming to light; and it was now resolved that the matter should be brought into the notice of the judicial authority at an early day.

The only circumstance which I have further occasion to notice, related to a diversion which was not unusual at that day amongst the inhabitants of the province, and which required the permission of the Council. It was brought into debate by Colonel Talbot.

"Stark Whittle, the swordsman," he said, "has challenged Sergeant Travers to play a prize at such weapons as they may select—and the Sergeant accepts the challenge, provided it meet the pleasure of his Lordship and the Council. I promised to be a patron to the play."

"It shall be as you choose," said the Proprietary. "This martial sport has won favour with our people. Let it be so ordered that it tend not to the breach of the peace. We commit it to your hands, Colonel Talbot." The Council, assented and the necessary order was recorded on the journal.

CHAPTER XVII

Some do call me Jack, sweetheart,
And some do call me Jille:
But when I come to the king's faire courte,
They call me Wilfulle Wille.

The Knight and Shepherd's Daughter.

The Skipper's necessary affairs in the port engaged him all the day succeeding that of his interview with father Pierre, and therefore prevented him from making his intended visit to the Cripple of St. Jerome's. When the next morning broke upon him, the early bell of St. Mary's Chapel informed him of the Sabbath,—a day seldom distinguished in his calendar from the rest of the week. It was, however, not unheeded now, as it suggested the thought that an opportunity might be afforded him to gain a sight of Blanche Warden—and even, perchance an interview—at the service of the Chapel. In this hope he at once relinquished his design of going to St. Jerome's, at least until after the morning offices of the church were performed. Accordingly, at an hour somewhat in advance of the general attendance of the congregation, the Skipper was seen loitering in the purlieus of the Chapel, where he marked with an inquisitive but cautious watchfulness the various groups that were coming to their devotions. When at length his strained vision was able to descry a cavalcade approaching from the direction of St. Inigoe's, and he discerned the figures of Albert Verheyden and Blanche Warden dallying far in the rear of the Collector and his daughter Alice, their horses almost at a walk, and themselves manifestly engrossed in an earnest conference, he turned hastily towards the church and with a compressed lip and knitted brow, ascended the stair and threw himself into an obscure corner of the little gallery which looked upon the altar. Here he remained a sullen and concealed observer of the rites of the temple,—his bosom rankling with uncharitable thoughts, and his countenance clouded with feelings the most ungenial to the lowly self-abasement and contrition of heart which breathed in every word of the solemn ritual that addressed his ear.

The Collector's family entered the place of worship. The Secretary still accompanied Blanche, knelt beside her in prayer, opened her missal to the various services of the day, and tendered the customary offices of familiar gallantry common to such an occasion, with an unrebuked freedom: all this in the view of the Skipper, whose eye flashed with a vengeful fire, as he gazed upon the man to whom he attributed the wrong he deemed himself to have suffered in his recent interview with the maiden. The service ended and the throng was retiring, when Cocklescraft planted himself on the outside of the door. His purpose was to exchange even but a word with the daughter of the Collector—at least to win a recognition of his presence by a smile, a nod, the smallest courtesy,—so dear to the heart of a lover. She came at last, loiteringly with father Pierre and Albert Verheyden. Perhaps she did not see Cocklescraft in the shade of the big elm, even although her father's weaker sight had recognised him, and the old man had stepped aside to shake his hand. She passed on to her horse without once turning her head towards him. The Skipper abruptly sprang from the Collector to help her into her saddle, but Blanche had already Albert's hand, and in a moment was in her seat. Cocklescraft's proffered service was acknowledged by a bow and only a casual word. The Secretary in an instant mounted his steed, and, with the maiden, set forth on their ride at a brisk gallop. The Brother of the Coast forgetful of his usual circumspection, stood with folded arms and moody visage, looking darkly upon them as they disappeared, and muttering half-audible ejaculations of wrath. He was, after an interval, roused from his abstraction by the hand of father Pierre gently laid upon his shoulder:

"You have forgotten the censer of virgin silver, you promised to offer at this shrine," said the priest in a grave voice. "It was to be an offering for the sin of a wayward spirit of anger. Beware, son, that thou dost no wrong to a brother."

"I have not forgotten the censer, holy father," returned the Skipper, with an ineffectual effort to assume his usual equanimity. "I have only deferred the offering—until I may give it," he added in a stern voice—"with an honest conscience. Thou shalt have it anon. I have business now that stands in the way:—good morning to you, father." And with these words he walked rapidly away.

In the afternoon Cocklescraft was seen plying his way from the quay in a small boat, attended by two seamen who rowed him to a point some five or six miles below the town, where he landed, and set out on foot for St. Jerome's.

On the following morning, whilst the dawn yet cast its grey hue over the face of the land, two men, in shaggy frize dresses, arrived at the hut of the Cripple. They rode on rough, little beach-ponies, each provided with a sack. The mastiff bitch eyed the visiters with a malign aspect from her station beneath the door sill, and by her low mutterings warned them against a too near approach. They accordingly stood at bay.

"Curse on the slut!" said one; "she has the eye of a very devil;—it might not be safe to defy her. Not a mouse is stirring:—the old Trencherman is as still as his bowl. Were it safe, think you, to wake him?"

"Why not?" demanded the other. "He will be in a passion, and threaten, at first, with his weapon;—but when he knows we come to trade with him, I will warrant he butters his wrinkles as smoothly with a smile as you could desire. Strike your staff, Nichol, against the door."

"The fiend fetch me, if I venture so near as to strike, with that bitch at the step. Try it thyself, Perry Cadger."

"Nay, and it comes to that, I will rouse him in another fashion," said the other.

"Master Swale—Master Robert Swale—Halloo—halloo!"

"Rob, man, awake,—turn out for thy friends!" exclaimed the first. The growl of the mastiff bitch was now changed into a hoarse bark. Some stir was heard from the inside of the hut, and, in a moment afterwards, the door was unbolted and brought sufficiently open to allow the uncouth head and half dressed figure of the Cripple to be seen. A short blunderbuss was levelled directly in the face of the visiters, whilst an ungracious repulse was screamed out in a voice husky with rage.

"Begone, you misbegotten thieves! What makes you here? Do you think I am an ale draper to take in every strolling runagate of the night. Begone, or by my body, I will baptize you with a sprinkling of lead!"

"In God's name, Robert Swale," exclaimed the first speaker, "turn thy weapon aslant! Thou mayst do a deed of mischief upon thy friends. We are Nichol Upstake, and Peregrine Cadger—friends, Rob,—friends, who have come to drive bargains to thy profit. Open your eyes, Master—put on your glasses—we have gold in pocket, man."

"Ha, ha, ha!" chuckled the tenant of the hut; "thou art astir, cronies! Ha, ha! I took ye for land loupers—sharks. By the Five Wounds, I knew ye not! Have patience a space and I will open."

When the Cripple had dressed himself he came swinging forth in his bowl, and passing beyond the curtilage of his dwelling went to the beach, whither he was followed by his two visiters who had now dismounted from their ponies. Here he halted, and taking off his cap, exposed his bare head and loose white tresses to the morning breeze which came somewhat sharply from the water.

"Soh!" he exclaimed, "there is refreshment in that! It is my custom to expel these night-cap vapours with the good salt water breeze: that is a commodity that may reach the province without paying duty to his Lordship! a cheap physic, a cheap physic, masters. Now what scent art thou upon, Nichol Upstake? Perry Cadger, man of sarsnet and grogram, I guess thy errand."

"In truth, Robert Swale," said Upstake— —

"No Robert Swale, nor Master Robert Swale," testily interrupted the owner of the cabin: "none of your worshipful phrase for me! Thou art but a shallow hypocrite to affect this reverence. Rob of the Bowl is the best I get from you when your longings are satisfied; ay, and it is said with a curl of your lip; and you make merry over my unworthiness with your pot-fellows. So, be honest, and give me plain Rob; I seek no flattery."

"You do us wrong, good Master Rob," interposed Peregrine Cadger— —

"To your needs," said Rob, sternly: "Speak in the way of your trade! You have no voice, nor I ear for aught else."

"Then, in brief," said Nichol Upstake, "I would fain know if you could supply me with Antigua to-day, or aqua vitæ, I care not which?"

"If such a thing might be, where wouldst thou take it, Nichol?" inquired Rob.

"To Warrington on the Cliffs."

"Ay, to Warrington on the Cliffs; good!—and warily to be borne? no hawk's eye upon thy path?"

"It shall be by night, if you like it," said the dealer.

"Well, well!" replied the Cripple; "I can give you a little of both, master: a flagon or so; some three or four. My hut is small, and hath a scant cellar. But the money in hand, Nichol Upstake! Good gold—full weight—and a fair price, too, mark you! I must have a trifle above my last market—ten shillings the gallon on the brandy, and two more for the Antigua. Leave thy kegs, and see me again at sunset. The money in hand! the money in hand! there is no trust in my commonwealth."

"It shall be so," said Nichol.

"And now, Master Cadger, what wilt? You have a scheme to cozen dame and wench with gewgaws; I see it in thine eye: and you will swear upon book and cross, if need be, they have stood you a wondrous hard purchase, even at the full three hundred per cent. excess you purpose to exact above the cost; and all the while it has come out of Rob's warehouse as cheap as beggars' alms: Ha, ha, ha! This world thrives on honesty! it grows fat on virtue! knavery only starves! Your rogue in rags, what hath he but his deserts! Let him repent and turn virtuous, like you and me, Perry, and his torn cloak and threadbare doublet shall be fenced and lined to defy all weathers. Hark ye, master, I have camblets, satins, and velvets, cambric, and lawn for thee—choice commodities all. Thou shalt see them in the hut."

"How came you by so rich an inventory, Rob?"

The Cripple turned a fierce eye upon the mercer, and with one glance conveyed his meaning, as he touched the handle of his dagger and said in a low tone,

"Dost forget the covenant between us? Peregrine Cadger you know I brook no such question."

The mercer stood for a moment abashed, and then replied: "An idle word, Master Rob, which meant no harm: as you say, honesty will only thrive. You shall find never a knave that is not some part fool. I will into the hut to look at the wares."

"Do so," said the Cripple. "You will find them in the box behind the door. There is need that you leave me, so follow him, Nichol. I have sudden business, masters, which it does not concern you to witness. When you have seen what you desire, depart quickly; leave your sacks and come back at sunset. I charge you, have a care that your eyes do not wander towards my motions. You know me, and know that I have sentinels upon your steps who have power to sear your eye-balls if you but steal one forbidden glance: away!"

The dealers withdrew into the hut, wondering at the abrupt termination of their interview, and implicitly confiding in the power of the Cripple to make good his threat.

"The Lord have mercy upon us!" said the mercer, in a smothered voice, after they had entered the door; "the Cripple hath matters on hand which it were not for our good to pry into. Pray you, Nichol, let us make our survey and do his bidding, by setting forth at once. I am not the man to give him offence."

The cause of this unexpected dismissal of the visiters was the apparition of Cocklescraft, whose figure, in the doubtful light of the morning, was seen by Rob at a distance, on the profile of the bank in the neighbourhood of the Wizard's Chapel. He had halted upon observing the Cripple in company with strangers, and had made a signal which was sufficiently intelligible to the person to whom it was addressed, to explain his wish to meet him.

Rob, having thus promptly rid himself of his company, now swung on his short crutches, almost as rapidly as a good walker could have got over the ground, towards the spot where the Buccaneer had halted.

"Steer your cockleshell there to the right, old worm!" said the Freebooter, as Rob came opposite to the bank on which he stood. "You shall find it easier to come up by the hollow."

"The plagues of a foul conscience light on thee!" replied the Cripple, desisting from farther motion, and wiping the perspiration from his brow. "Is it more seemly I should waste my strength on the fruitless labour to clamber up that rough slope, or thou come down to me? You mock me, sirrah!" he added, with an expression of sudden anger; "Thou know'st I cannot mount the bank."

"Thou know'st I can drag thee up, reverend fragment of a sinful man!" returned Cocklescraft, jocularly; "yes, and with all thy pack of evil passions at thy back, besides. Would you hold our meeting in sight from the window of the hut, where you have just lodged a pair of your busy meddlers—your bumpkin cronies in the way of trade? It was such as these that, but a few nights ago, set his Lordship's hounds upon our tracks. Come up, man, without farther parley."

The Cripple's fleeting anger changed, as usual, to that bitter smile and chuckle with which he was wont to return into a tractable mood, as he said,—

"A provident rogue! a shrewd imp! He has his instinct of mischief so keen that his forecast never sleepeth. The devil hath made him a perfect scholar. There, Dickon, give me thy hand," he added, when he came to the steep ascent which his machine of locomotion was utterly inadequate to surmount. "Give me thy hand, good cut-throat. Help me to the top."

The muscular seaman, instead of extending his hand to his companion, descended the bank, and taking the bowl and its occupant upon his shoulder, strode upward to the even ground, and deposited his load with as little apparent effort as if he had been dealing with a truss of hay.

"Bravely!" ejaculated Rob, when he was set down. "I scarce could have done better in my best day. Now, what set thee to jogging so early, Dickon? Where dost thou come from?"

"From the Chapel," replied the other. "I came there from the Port last night, express to see you; and having no special favour for the bed I slept on, I left it at the first streak of light to go and rouse you from your dreams, and lo! there you are at one of your dog and wolf bargains with the country side clowns."

"Discreet knaves, Dickon, who have come to ease us of somewhat of our charge of contraband: stout jerkins—stout and well lined; rogues of substance—Nichol Upstake, the ordinary keeper of Warrington, and Perry Cadger, the mercer of St. Mary's. Seeing thee here, I dismissed them until sunset. That Peregrine Cadger is somewhat leaky as a gossip, and might tell tales if he were aware that I consorted with you."

"I see them taking the road on their ponies," said Cocklescraft; "we may venture to the hut. I am sharp set for breakfast, and when I have a contented stomach, I will hold discourse with you, Rob, touching matters of some concern to us both."

The Cripple and his guest, upon this hint, repaired to the hut, and in due time the morning meal was supplied and despatched. Cocklescraft then opened the purport of his visit.

"Has it ever come into your wise brain, Master Rob," he asked, "that you are getting somewhat old; and that it might behoove you to make a shrift at the confessional, by way of settling your account? I take it, it will not be a very clean reckoning without a good swashing penance."

"How now, thou malignant kite!" exclaimed the Cripple; "what's in the wind?"

"Simply, Rob, that the time has come when, peradventure, we must part. I am tired of this wicked life. I shall amend; and I come to counsel you to the like virtuous resolution. I will be married, Robert Swale, Man of the Bowl!"

"Grammercy! thou wilt be married! thou! I spit upon thee for a fool. What crotchet is this?"

"I will be married, as I say, neither more nor less. Now to what wench, ask you? Why to the very fairest and primest flower of this province—the Rose of St. Mary's—the Collector's own daughter. I mark that devil's sneer of unbelief of yours, old buckler man: truer word was never spoke by son of the sea or land, than I speak now."

"To the Collector's daughter!" ejaculated the Cripple, in a tone of derision. "Thy carriage is bold in the Port, but no measure of audacity will ever bring thee to that favour. Would'st thou play at thine old game, and sack the town, and take the daintiest in it for ransom? You know no other trick of wooing, Dickon."

"By my hand, Rob, I am specially besought by the Collector to make one at a choice merry-making which his daughter has on foot for next Thursday. Ay, and I am going, on his set command, to dance a gailliard with Mistress Blanche. Oh, she shall be the very bird of the sea—the girl of the billow, Rob! She shall be empress of the green wave that nursed me, and the blue sky, and the wide waste. Her throne shall be on the deck of my gay bark: and my merry men shall spring at her beck as deftly as at the boatswain's pipe!"

"You shall sooner meet your deservings," said Rob, "on the foal of the acorn, with a hempen string, than find grace with the Collector's child. Thy whole life has been adversary to the good will of the father."

"I know it," replied Cocklescraft. "I was born in natural warfare with the customs and all who gather them; the more praise for my exploit! I shall change my ways and forsake evil company. I shall be a man of worship. We shall shut up the Chapel, Rob; expel our devils; pack off our witches to Norway, and establish an honest vocation. Therefore, Rob, go to father Pierre; repent of your misdeeds, and live upon your past gains. You are rich and may afford to entertain henceforth a reputable conscience."

"Do not palter with me, sirrah! but tell me what this imports."

"Then truly, Rob, I am much disturbed in my fancies. I love the wench, and mean to have her—fairly if I can—but after the fashion of the Coast if I must. She doth not consent as yet—mainly because she hath a toy of delight in that silken Secretary of my Lord—a bookish pale-cheeked, sickly strummer of stringed instruments—one Master Verheyden, I think they call him."

"Ha!" exclaimed the Cripple, as a frown gathered on his brow; "what is he? Whence comes he?"

"His Lordship's chamber secretary," replied Cocklescraft; "brought hither I know not when nor whence. A silent-paced, priestly pattern of modesty, who feeds on the favour of his betters, as a lady's dog, that being allowed to lick the hand of his mistress, takes the privilege to snarl on all who approach her. I shall make light work with him by whipping him out of my way. Why are you angry, that you scowl so, Master Rob?"

"I needs must be angry to see thee make a fool of thyself," replied the master of the hut. "Verheyden—his Lordship's secretary!" he muttered to himself. "No, no! it would be a folly to think it."

"Mutter as you will, Rob," said Cocklescraft; "by St. Iago, I will try conclusions with the Secretary—folly or no folly! He hath taught the maiden," he added, with a bitter emphasis, "to affect a scorn for me, and he shall smart for it."

"Ha! thy spirit is ever for undoing!" exclaimed Rob, suddenly changing his mood, and forcing a harsh laugh of derision. "Mischief is your proper element—your food, your repose, your luxury. Well, if thou needst must take on a new life, and strive to be worshipful, I would counsel thee to begin it with some deed of charity, not strife. I had as well make my lecture to a young wolf! Ha, Dickon, thou wilt be a prospering pupil to the master that teaches thee the virtue of charity! Such rede will be welcome to thee as water to thy shoes! I have scanned thee in all thy humours!"

"I spurn upon your advice, and will not be scorned, old man!" said Cocklescraft, angrily. "The maiden shall be mine, though I pluck her from beneath her father's blazing roof-tree; and then farewell to the province, and to thee! Mark you that! I come not to be taunted with thy ill-favoured speech! My men shall be withdrawn from the Chapel. I will put them on worthier service than to minister to thy greediness."

"Hot-brained, silly idiot—thou drivelling fool!" shouted Rob. "Dost thou not know that I can put thee in the dust and trample on thee as a caitiff? that I can drive thee from the province as a vile outlaw? Art thou such a dizzard as to tempt my anger? If you would thrive even in your villanous wooing, have a care not to provoke my displeasure! One word from me, and not a man paces thy deck: thou goest abroad unattended, stiverless—a fugitive, with hue and cry at thy heels. How dar'st thou reprove me, boy?"

"Thy hand, Rob," said Cocklescraft, relenting. "You say no more than my folly warrants; I am a wanton fool: your pardon—let there be peace between us."

"Art reasonable again? Bravely confessed, Dickon! I forgive thy rash speech. Now go thy ways, and the Foul One speed thee! I have naught to counsel, either for strife or peace, since thou hast neither wit, wisdom, nor patience for sober advice against the current of thy will. It will not be long before this maimed trunk shall sink into its natural resting place—and it matters not to me how my remnant of time be spent—whether in hoarding or keeping. The world will find me an heir to squander what little store it hath pleased my fortune to gather. So go thy ways!"

"I will see you again, friend Rob," said the Buccaneer. "I have matter to look after at the Chapel, and then shall get back to the Port, to drive my suit to a speedy issue. I came here but in honest dealing with you, to give you friendly notice of my design, and, perchance, to get your aid. You have no counsel for me? It is well; my own head and arm shall befriend me; they have stood me in stead in straits more doubtful than this: farewell—farewell!"

As the Skipper stepped along the beach, Rob planted himself in the door of the hut and looked after him for some moments, nodding his head significantly towards him, and muttering in a cynical undertone, "Go thy ways, snake of the sea, spawn of a water devil! Thou married! ha, ha! Thy lady gay shall have a sweetened cup in thee: and thy wooing shall be tender and gentle—yea, as the appetite of the sword-fish. It shall be festival wooing—all in the light—in the light—of the bride's own blazing roof: a dainty wolf! a most tractable shark! Oh, I cannot choose but laugh!"